Ronald Hillary is a graduate of Central Michigan University with a business degree in Marketing and an MBA in Management. After various sales positions, he founded a commercial printing company located in Grand Rapids, whose sales territory covered most of Western Michigan.

His interest in the game of golf began when he was an eleven-year-old caddy at a private country club located two blocks from his family's home. His love of the game has continued to this day and his fascination with The Masters Tournament was the direct inspiration for the writing of this book.

For my wife, Rosalind, who has battled multiple sclerosis for fifty-one years with grace and the most amazing, optimistic determination that I could have ever only imagined. She has truly been my inspiration.

Ronald Hillary

THE TOURNAMENT

AUSTIN MACAULEY PUBLISHERS™

LONDON • CAMBRIDGE • NEW YORK • SHARJAH

Copyright © Ronald Hillary (2021)

All rights reserved. No part of this publication may be reproduced, distributed, or transmitted in any form or by any means, including photocopying, recording, or other electronic or mechanical methods, without the prior written permission of the publisher, except in the case of brief quotations embodied in critical reviews and certain other noncommercial uses permitted by copyright law. For permission requests, write to the publisher.

Any person who commits any unauthorized act in relation to this publication may be liable to criminal prosecution and civil claims for damages.

This is a work of fiction. Names, characters, businesses, places, events, locales, and incidents are either the products of the author's imagination or used in a fictitious manner. Any resemblance to actual persons, living or dead, or actual events is purely coincidental.

Ordering Information
Quantity sales: Special discounts are available on quantity purchases by corporations, associations, and others. For details, contact the publisher at the address below.

Publisher's Cataloging-in-Publication data
Hillary, Ronald
The Tournament

ISBN 9781647502423 (Paperback)
ISBN 9781647502430 (Hardback)
ISBN 9781647502447 (ePub e-book)

Library of Congress Control Number: 2021906322

www.austinmacauley.com/us

First Published (2021)
Austin Macauley Publishers LLC
40 Wall Street, 33rd Floor, Suite 3302
New York, NY 10005
USA

mail-usa@austinmacauley.com
+1 (646) 5125767

I would like to thank and acknowledge those that have encouraged me and have had a direct impact in the development of this book.

Colleen Weber – Owner of Mi Design LLC, located in Wayland, Michigan, she was of extraordinary help in turning my handwritten pages into workable, typeset chapters. Colleen not only helped with the basic typesetting process but also offered proofreading and made suggestions that moved the story along.

Joseph J. Hesse – Joe, my good friend and golfing buddy, took the time to read the early manuscripts and offered meaningful suggestions and guidance, which had a direct impact on the story and character development. I can't thank you enough, Joseph.

Fr. Leonard A. Sudlik – Just when I thought the book was complete, my parish priest and longtime golfing partner mentioned that he "would like to know more about how the main character (JD) qualified to play in The Masters Tournament." As a result, I then had to develop the storyline for The Qualifier and then the playing in The U.S. Amateur Championship. I am thankful for his suggestion, as I feel this background information added a necessary element to the overall story. Thank you, Fr. Len.

Prologue
The Qualifier

Qualifying for the U.S. Amateur Golf Championship is very difficult. Most amateur players never make the attempt. Nor do they even dream of accomplishing such a task. However, after much discussion with his golf instructor, Andy Van Lear, and Patrick Davis, the grandfather who raised him from the age of three and the one who introduced him to the game, it was decided that JD, as he was known to his friends and family, would make the effort.

John David Andrews (JD) was the one who first approached both men with the idea of competing in this national tournament. At first, they both tried to discourage him, expressing their thoughts of his being so young, only fifteen years old, that it was too soon for him to attempt to compete at such a high level.

Convincing them, however, did not take too much effort. After reviewing the progress he had made playing junior tournaments over the past three years, the number he had won and the ease with which he had won them, they agreed to help by researching how he would go about qualifying for that year's U.S. Amateur Championship.

It was the 1st of May, 1957. Sitting in his grandfather's living room, JD looked at his golf instructor and his grandfather and asked, "So, how do I go about qualifying for the U.S. Amateur?" With a slight smile, Andy Van Lear cleared his throat and proceeded to explain what they had to do.

"First, JD, you will have to enter a qualifying tournament. I have made some phone calls. The closest sectional qualifying site to us here in Grand Rapids, Michigan, will be held at the Country Club of Lansing. It is only a one-hour drive, so we won't have to stay in a hotel. We can drive home and then drive back for the second round, the next day. There is a fee of $75.00 to enter the event plus covering our expenses, such as lunch and snacks."

Looking at his grandson, Patrick spoke up, "JD, we can certainly cover these costs, if you really want to try this."

Looking first at his grandfather and then at his golf instructor, JD responded, "I would really like to go and see if I am good enough to play at that level. When do they play the qualifying rounds?"

"Well, the qualifier is held this July 16th and 17th, and begins at 8 a.m. It's a 36-hole stroke play competition with five qualifying spots, plus two alternate positions up for advancement to the Amateur Championship. If we all agree, Patrick, you can write the check for the entry fee and I will send it with the official entry forms."

With both his grandfather and JD nodding their heads yes, Andy said, "OK then, let's do it!"

The next ten weeks seemed to go by in a flash. During this time, JD did play in two local tournaments, winning one by six strokes and losing one in a three-hole play-off. He felt good about his game and was looking forward to the trip to Lansing, especially because both his grandfather and his golf instructor would be with him.

When July 16th came, Andy pulled up to Patrick's house in his Chevy station wagon and announced, "I will drive because this car will give us room for the three of us, plus JD's clubs and the cooler of sandwiches and drinks that I took the liberty of bringing." Thanking Andy, JD and Patrick got in the car and they began the drive to the Country Club of Lansing.

Patrick looked at his watch and announced, "It's 5 a.m., if all goes well, we should arrive a little after six which will give us time to check-in, get our tee-time, and JD, you can warm-up on the practice range." With that said, they settled in for what would prove to be an easy drive.

Glancing at JD in the back seat, Patrick noticed his grandson seemed to be asleep. Chuckling, he nudged Andy and pointed at JD. Andy shook his head and kept driving.

The drive seemed short, although it did take a full sixty minutes. Arriving at the Country Club of Lansing, they were directed to a parking lot set aside for the players and from there they were escorted to the 'Entrants Tent.' Once the check-in formalities were completed, JD and Andy walked to the practice range while Patrick went in search of the men's facilities.

Having been informed that his tee-time was 8:30, JD had a solid hour to spend on the driving range with extra time to practice his putting stroke on the practice green. Andy Van Lear was satisfied with JD's warm-up. His stroke looked good and he seemed to be relaxed and ready. Watching his practice putts, Andy approached, "JD, let the putter head flow through the ball and make a smooth stroke." Once he was confident his player was ready, he looked at his watch and said, "Time to make our way to the first tee."

Picking up his equipment, JD smiled at Andy and remarked, "I feel good, I think I am as ready as I can be."

"Good, JD, just go out and play your normal game, you are ready."

While they were walking to the first tee, Patrick approached them and had his grandson put a couple of ham sandwiches and two cokes in his bag, saying, "Be sure to eat one sandwich and drink one coke on each of the nine holes. This will help you maintain the energy you will need for the day." Thanking his grandfather and Andy for all their help, JD turned and shouldering his bag, walked to the first tee.

He noticed that his fellow competitors were occupied with their own thoughts and final preparations, so JD took a few moments to look around and take in the beauty of one of the finest country clubs in Michigan.

The Country Club of Lansing was founded in 1908. After the initial start-up and operating for the first 12 years, the directors decided to hire a golf architect to design and lay out a professional 18-hole course. So, in 1920, the founders contracted William Langford, a nationally known golf course architect, to make their dream of a first-class country club, come to fruition. Under his guidance, the current 18 holes were developed. What JD observed were tree-lined fairways, bunkers of white sand, and the two greens that he could see from the first tee-box seemed to have a significantly sloped look.

Turning back to the other players, JD introduced himself and the starter announced the order of play and the parameters of the event. "Young men, this is the first round of a sectional qualifier for playing in this year's U.S. Amateur Championship. It is a 36-hole, stroke play competition. You are playing for five qualifying spots, plus two alternate positions up for advancement to the championship that will be held this year at the Medinah Country Club located just outside the city of Chicago, Illinois. All rules of the U.S.G.A. (United States Golf Association) are in play. Does anyone have any questions?" No questions were asked, so the starter motioned to player number one, saying, "You may proceed to tee-off."

Once the first two players had hit their drives, it was JD's turn. He calmly teed his ball, took a practice swing, and proceeded to drive his ball down the center of the fairway. Under the rules of golf, no one is allowed to offer any advice, other than a player's caddy, that would help the golfer in any way. Because of this rule, Patrick and Andy could only walk along and observe the match from a discreet distance.

JD played steady golf and so did his two playing companions. When the round was over, he posted a score of 68, four shots under the course par of 72, having shot six birdies and two bogies. Once he had posted the score and it was verified for accuracy, he left the scorer's tent to find his grandfather and golf instructor waiting. "That was a good round," Andy said, "Let's put your clubs in the car, eat a sandwich and then make the drive home." Patrick and JD thought that was a good idea, so they took the cooler from the back of Andy's station wagon, dropped the back wagon door and sat on it while they had their lunch.

During lunch, Andy asked JD about the round. "How did you find the course? Was there anything about the layout that you found especially difficult?"

"Not really," replied JD.

"Well then, young man, let's wrap up, drive home and get a good night's rest. We will call from Grand Rapids and get your tee-time for tomorrow. I will drive again and we will do a repeat of the trip we took today."

"Thank you, Andy," said Patrick.

"Yes, thank you both," said JD.

All were tired, so the drive home was a quiet one. Once they arrived, Andy used Patrick's phone to contact the people in charge of the tournament and was informed that JD's tee-time for the second qualifying round was set for 8:50 a.m. After thanks all around, Andy said he would pick Patrick and JD up at 5 a.m. "You played well today. Try to get a good night's sleep and I will see you both tomorrow morning."

JD did sleep fairly well. Even so, when the alarm clock went off, he thought that the night had passed too quickly.

When Patrick opened his bedroom door, JD greeted him with a, "Good morning, Grandpa, I'm ready to go as soon as you are."

Smiling at his grandson, he said, "Maybe we should eat some breakfast before Andy arrives."

"Okay, I guess I'm just a little anxious to get going."

"I'm sure you are, but first things first. Andy will be here in about thirty minutes."

Twenty minutes later, the station wagon pulled up in front of Patrick's house. Patrick and JD came out of the side door, walked down the narrow driveway and got into the car. Once they were past the city limits, the miles seemed to pass quickly. JD was not sleeping and both men noticed that he was staring out the side window with a pensive look on his face.

"What's the matter, JD, are you worried about the match? You know that there are five qualifying spots and two alternate positions to advance to the Amateur Championship. Your play yesterday puts you right in position for one of those. So, don't worry about anything. Let Andy and me do the worrying. You just go out and play your best."

"Thanks, Grandpa, I just don't want to let you down."

"If you give it your best, you will never let us down."

After that exchange, JD calmed down and started to think about the course and which holes might be particularly difficult.

Arriving, they drove to the players' parking area and unloaded their gear. JD's clubs, shoes and golf cap as well as the cooler of drinks and sandwiches. Sliding the side zipper of his bag down, JD put two sandwiches and four cokes into his bag. Securing the zipper in its up position, he put on his golf shoes and cap, shouldered the bag, and walked with Andy to check-in, telling his grandfather that, "We will be at the range loosening up."

"Well, I will make a rest stop and see you and Andy there before your tee-time."

Checking in, JD was handed a players list, with his tee-time of 8:50 a.m. circled.

Andy looked relieved. "I could not get through to the club when I called this morning, so I'm glad to see that we have plenty of time to warm-up."

Smiling at his golf instructor, JD responded, "Let's make the most of it."

They then made their way to the practice area. While JD was hitting his practice shots, Andy looked over the players sheet that JD had been given when he checked-in. The second-round list of golfers was considerably less than it had been for the first round. Ninety-six had advanced, but there were eight who had withdrawn and four had been listed as no-shows, leaving eighty-four who would play for the right to advance to the Amateur Championship.

Finishing his warm-up, JD asked Andy, "What time is it?"

"Eight-thirty and we should make our way to the first tee."

Just as they were leaving the practice range, Patrick joined them. When they reached the first tee, JD turned and gave his grandfather a long, firm hug. Whispering to him, "Thanks, Grandpa, for being here with me."

"Oh, I wouldn't miss this for the world, JD. Now, just play your best and enjoy the competition."

Turning to Andy, he also gave him a warm embrace, thanking him for being there. Picking up his bag, he walked to the tee area where he was introduced to the other 8:50 a.m. players.

By the luck of the draw, JD was first to tee-off. His swing had a fluid motion with the ball seeming to explode off of the club face. Picking up his tee, he waited for the other players to tee-off and then, shouldering his bag, began the walk down the first fairway.

Following his usual routine, JD took two practice swings and then stroked his second shot, to the center of the first green. Two putts later, he had his par. The round seemed to progress without any major mistakes until he reached #14. This hole had a pond just left of the green. JD hooked his second shot into the pond. After taking the penalty, his fourth shot, a somewhat difficult chip, hit the flagstick, which caused his ball to shoot right and roll off the front of the green. His next chip was close to the cup and he made the two-foot putt, resulting in a double-bogey six.

Andy and Patrick noticed that JD seemed to be muttering to himself. "Let's hope he shakes that off," Andy said to Patrick.

"Well, we'll see how his nerves are now, Andy."

JD seemed to settle down after his drive off the 15th tee. Once again he settled into a solid routine and it looked like he had shrugged off the misfortune.

However, standing on the 17th tee, a par three hole, JD stared at a pond that was located to the right of the green. For some reason, that he later was not able to explain, JD pushed his iron shot right into the middle of the pond. After his penalty drop, his approach chip onto the green and two putts, he had another double bogey. He then proceeded to par #18. For a player of JD's caliber, it was a very sloppy finish to what had been a solid round for the first thirteen holes.

Posting his score of 76, bringing his two-day total to 144, he went in search of his grandfather. He didn't have to go far. Patrick and Andy were waiting for him just outside of the roped-off area that led to the scoring tent.

"I'm sorry, I kind of lost my focus after the double bogey on 14."

Putting an arm around his shoulder, Patrick responded by saying, "JD, we can't always control the way the ball bounces, but I am proud of you for the effort you made over these last two days."

Andy spoke up, "Well, it looks like we have to stick around. I have checked the leaderboard and your score of even par might get you into a play-off."

Andy's comment turned out to be prophetic. After all the scores had been posted, the first-place score for the 36-hole total was 134. Second was 137 and third was 139. That left four players tied at an even par total of 144. There was going to be a sudden death play-off to secure the final two spots plus the two alternate positions. JD still had a chance to qualify for the Amateur Championship. There wasn't much time between the last players finishing and the start of the play-off. Andy made sure JD had a sandwich and a couple of Coca-Cola's. They then went to the practice range to hit a few balls to stay loose.

The play-off was not the first one for JD. He had been in four junior tournament play-offs over the last two years. He had won three and lost one. So, he was not particularly nervous about trying to secure a qualifying spot.

When play started, one of the four players birdied the first hole, winning the fourth qualifying spot. The second hole was played by the remaining three and all shot par and had to go back to the first tee and start the process again.

The scoring, playing the first hole for the third time that day, was unusual. One player birdied, securing the final qualifying spot. JD got his par, which secured the first alternate position while the third player became the second alternate with a bogey five. The drive home was a quiet one. Finally, about a half-hour from Patrick's house, JD spoke up.

"Well, I guess that's that."

"Not necessarily, JD," it was Andy who had responded. "You are the first alternate and it is possible that something could happen to one of the qualifiers."

"Andy's right, JD. Why don't we just settle in, get a good night's sleep and see what happens."

"Okay, Grandpa, I will go to work tomorrow at the Lincoln Golf Course and continue to work on my game."

Andy and Patrick smiled at each other.

"That's the JD I know," said Patrick. Five days later, Patrick received a call in the early evening. One of the qualifiers had broken two fingers on his left hand while trying to remove a tree limb from his property and had to withdraw from the Amateur Championship. Because JD had finished as the first alternate, they wanted to know if he would be able to play. Assuring them he would, Patrick couldn't wait to let his grandson know they were going to Chicago.

The Amateur Championship

Patrick was sitting on his front step when JD arrived home from working at the Lincoln Golf Course. JD parked his bicycle, looked up and greeted his grandfather with a cheery, "Hi, Grandpa."

"Hi yourself, JD. Guess what?"

"Something good, Grandpa?"

"Yes, you are in the U.S. Amateur Championship. I received a phone call this afternoon and one of the qualifiers had an accident and cannot play. So, as first alternate, you are in."

"Wow, have you told Mr. Van Lear?"

"Not yet, JD. But I think we should call him this evening. We only have four weeks to get ready. The Championship is played in August, over a full seven days. So, as your guardian, I will submit the entry form with a check for the $90.00 fee."

"That sounds great. Will you be able to take the time off from work? How will we get there? Where will we stay?"

"Slow down. Yes, I can take the time off. I will take my vacation and we will drive to Chicago."

"But, Grandpa, where will we stay?"

"I have some ideas, JD. Let's have dinner first and then call Andy. After that, we can work out the details. It might take me a week to put everything together, but you are definitely going to play in the Amateur Championship."

Giving his grandfather a big hug, JD could only say, "Thanks, Grandpa, you are the best and I don't know how to thank you enough."

"I love you, son, and it makes me very happy to see you have this opportunity."

Once dinner was finished and the kitchen was cleaned, Patrick placed the call to Andy Van Lear.

"Andy, JD is in the Amateur Championship. One of the qualifiers had an accident and broke his hand. So, JD is in."

"That's great news for us, Patrick. However, that leaves us with only four weeks to prepare, so I will have to work with JD more than usual to get him ready."

"Okay, I will work on making the arrangements in Chicago and thank you, Andy, I really appreciate all you have done for him."

"You're more than welcome, Patrick. I have never enjoyed myself more than the time JD and I have spent together, working on the game we both love."

After hanging up the phone, Patrick turned to his grandson, "Well, JD, Andy says you have a lot of work to do to get ready for the 'Amateur.' You will need to call him in the morning and work out a schedule. I will make our trip arrangements and send in your entry fee. It looks like I will be taking my vacation in August this year."

The next few weeks passed quickly. On the morning they were to leave for the drive to Chicago, JD asked, "Where are we going to stay?"

"Oh, do you remember when your grandmother's cousin stayed with us a couple of years ago?"

"Sure, his name is Ed Doyle, isn't it?"

"Yes, and he lives in Schaumburg, Illinois, which is a suburb of Chicago. I called and asked him for suggestions about where to stay and he invited us to stay with him. He said it is only a 40-minute drive to the Medinah Country Club, where the tournament is being held. I thanked him and accepted his invitation, so we won't have to stay in a hotel."

"That's great, Grandpa, I'll get my suitcase and golf bag. I should be ready in about 30 minutes."

After the car was loaded, JD and Patrick began the long drive to Schaumburg, Illinois. They had estimated it would take them about four hours driving time and it took all of that. It was around five in the afternoon, Sunday, August 23rd, when they finally pulled into Ed Doyle's driveway.

The tournament began the next day. It was being held at the Medinah Country Club, located in Medinah, Illinois. The club was founded in 1924 by the Shriners from Chicago's Medinah Temple. The Shriners describe themselves as a 'fraternity based on fun, fellowship, and the Masonic principles of brotherly love, relief, and truth.' Membership is open to men of integrity from all walks of life. The Shriners built a beautiful clubhouse with three eighteen-hole golf courses on 640 acres of land. The U.S. Amateur Championship was being played on course #3, a layout that was originally done by golf course designer, Tom Bendelow. This was followed up with A.W. Tillinghast playing a major role in design changes that were made to course # 3 in the 1930s.

After settling in, Patrick, JD, and Ed Doyle sat around Ed's dining room table catching up on family news and telling family stories that JD found fascinating. These were the type of things that he had missed, not having any relatives to share with. When the family stories finished, Patrick took out a file folder from a narrow briefcase that he had brought from home.

"JD, we need to review our schedule for the next week. Ed, if this will bore you, you really don't have to babysit us."

"Absolutely not, Patrick. I am fascinated that you have come here to have JD compete in such a prestigious tournament. I am going to listen and learn about what you are up against, young man."

Looking at Ed and his grandfather, JD said, "Okay, let's review our schedule. I only hope I can play well enough to complete all seven days."

"Well, we will just take it one day at a time, and Ed, thanks again for letting us stay with you."

"My pleasure, Patrick. Now, fill me in on what this tournament is all about."

Opening his file folder, Patrick began by reviewing the tournament schedule. "As you know, JD, the Amateur Championship is played over a full seven days. It is a combination of stroke play and match play, with a 36-hole final play-off to determine the winner. There are 312 players in the field. Monday and Tuesday are the stroke play days with 18 holes played each day. After those two rounds, the top 64 players advance to match play. Any ties that would allow more than 64 are settled with a sudden death play-off until the 64-player bracket is filled. On Wednesday, the #1 seeded player will play the #64 seeded player. This is how it is set up and at the end of the day, the field will be trimmed to 32 players. Again, any matches tied after 18 holes will be decided with sudden death play-offs.

"Thursday, 32 players will play in the morning. Sixteen will then play the afternoon matches, trimming the field down to eight. Friday, eight matches will trim the field to four. Saturday, four will play and the final two remaining players will advance to Sunday's final match. Sunday is a 36-hole event. Eighteen holes will be played in the morning, a lunch will be served, and then 18 additional holes will be played to determine the overall winner. Since it is match play, it does not have go the full 36-holes. Anytime one player is up more than there are holes left to play, the match is over and the winner declared. So, JD, I think you need to hit the sack and try to get a good night's sleep. We have a big day ahead of us and I hope a busy week after that."

Getting up from his chair, JD wrapped his arm around Patrick's shoulder and kissed him on the forehead. "Thanks, Grandpa, and thank you again, Mr. Doyle."

With that, JD went off to prepare for bed. Patrick and Ed stayed up for another hour talking and reviewing the schedule for the following seven days.

Finally, they both went to bed hoping that JD would be able to sleep and be ready for the championship.

The Monday and Tuesday rounds went well for JD. When Tuesday's rounds were finished, Patrick let him know that his combined scores of 147 had placed him in the top 64 that would advance to Wednesday's match play competition.

"JD, your play was good," Patrick told him. "You're not in the top 20 seeds, but you are in the 30th spot. So, you're going to be matched against the 35th seeded player. It's now match play. If you should have one bad hole, or even two, don't let it bother you. In match play, you can come back from a couple of high numbers. Just grind it out and let the chips fall where they may."

"I will, Grandpa, I will play my best through the whole match."

"That's all anyone can do and whatever happens, I want you to know how proud I am to have you as my grandson. Now, let's go back to Ed's house, grab some dinner, and rest up for tomorrow's match."

JD liked the match play format and his grandfather's take on the fact that one or two holes lost to double or triple bogey did not necessarily eliminate you from the tournament. A good player could fight his way back in by throwing pars and birdies at the opponent, coming from behind to win the match. This is exactly what happened during his Wednesday match. When it was over, JD had edged out a 2-up with one hole to play victory.

Arriving back at Ed Doyle's house, Patrick and JD each freshened up and while his grandson was taking a nap, Patrick called Andy Van Lear to let him know how JD was playing.

"Thanks for calling, Patrick. I was wondering how it was going. Tell JD I am pulling for him and I want to hear all about it when you get home."

"You can count on it, Andy. Why don't you come over to the house on Monday and I will let JD give you a blow-by-blow summary of the entire week."

"Sounds good, I'll be there around 7 p.m."

The Thursday and Friday matches fell JD's way, quicker and easier than he had expected. For some reason, his opponents did not seem to be on their game. He won Thursday's match 5-up with four to play and Friday's match 6-up with five to play. Saturday, however, proved to be a struggle. At the end of 18-holes, he was tied, even up, with his opponent. Neither player had been more than 1-up on each other during the entire match. When they found themselves dead even at the end of 18, they knew that they were now in a 'sudden death' play-off. After each player posted pars on their 19th, 20th and 21st holes, JD closed the match out by scoring a par 4 on the 22nd hole, while his opponent bogeyed the hole with a 1-over, par 5. JD was now in the final match on Sunday with a chance to win.

Sunday was a cooler, overcast day. Standing on the first tee, JD was introduced to his competitor, a young man of about 19 by the name of Perry Waldorf IV. When JD extended his hand to greet Perry, he was ignored. Somewhat taken aback, he heard Perry tell him, "Don't think you're going to beat me 'Muni' boy. I'm a member here and I'm way better than you."

JD was stunned. Never, in all the tournaments he had played, had anyone ever been so rude or said anything so nasty. Not quite knowing what to do, or how to respond, he just turned away and went to his bag to collect his driver and get ready to tee-off.

By virtue of the draw, Perry Waldorf IV had the tee. After hitting a long straight tee shot, he gave JD a look that basically said, 'Match that, boy!'

JD did match Perry's drive and every shot for the entire morning round.

Turning to the crowd of spectators, the tournament marshal announced, "After this morning's eighteen, the match is all square. We will now break for lunch and resume play at 1:30 this afternoon, to determine the winner and this year's U.S. Amateur Champion."

Patrick approached his grandson, "Well done, JD, let's get a good lunch and find a spot to rest a bit."

"Sounds good to me, Grandpa." JD did have a good lunch. He ordered a Philly steak sandwich, tossed salad with Thousand Island dressing, French fries, and a very large chocolate milkshake. Patrick smiled, remembering how he used to be able to eat like that. *Oh well,* he thought, as he took small bites of his tuna salad sandwich.

Leaving the dining room, they found a shady spot on the clubhouse veranda and just sat in silence for about 30 minutes. Turning to JD, Patrick pointed to his watch.

"Time to loosen up, JD, the match will start in about 50 minutes."

"OK, Grandpa. I'll get my clubs and meet you at the driving range."

Going through his usual routine, JD started with his wedges and proceeded to work his way through each club in his bag. Once he was finished with all but his driver, he walked over to the practice putting area. Satisfied with his putting stroke, he returned to the range and hit a dozen balls with his driver. Picking up his bag, he kept the driver in his hand.

"Well, Grandpa, I'm as ready as I can be. Let's see what this final eighteen brings."

"Good luck, JD, I will be with you all the way. Behind the ropes, of course, but with you nevertheless."

Once they had arrived at the first tee, JD once again approached Perry Waldorf IV to wish him well, but Perry turned his back on him and acted as if JD didn't even exist.

I guess I should have expected that, thought JD. Shaking the thought from his mind, he waited his turn and when it came, JD put his drive right down the middle of the first fairway, twenty yards past Perry's drive. Smiling to himself, JD thought, *OK, Perry, let the game begin.*

Throughout the afternoon, the match went back and forth. Once again, neither player could get much of a lead. Neither JD nor Perry could keep more than a one-up lead at any time.

Standing on the 18th tee, the match was all square. Both players had excellent drives. JD's second shot was wide right of the green. Perry's second found the right-side bunker. JD was away and he hit a good approach chip onto the green about fifteen feet from the hole. Walking toward the green, he stopped to give Perry time to hit his sand shot. During his backswing, Perry's club head brushed the sand.

This would be a two-stroke penalty during stroke play competition. However, JD and Perry were in the match play part of the tournament and the rule for match play is loss of hole. Additionally, because their match was tied and this was the final hole of the championship, the penalty would result in Perry losing the tournament.

Once Perry completed the shot, the ball came to rest three feet from the cup. He didn't bother raking the bunker, instead he walked onto the green and marked his ball. JD expected him to say something about his club brushing the sand, but Perry acted as if nothing unusual had happened.

JD took two putts to finish, scoring a 1-over par bogey five. Perry took one putt from three feet and pumped his fist in the air, exclaiming, "Yes, a par four and the win."

Now, JD was mad. He approached Perry and trying to control himself asked, "What about the penalty shot in the bunker?"

"What penalty shot?"

"Your club brushed the sand on your backswing, that's loss of hole and loss of match."

Looking JD right in the eyes, Perry said, "That didn't happen 'Muni' boy. I had a four and you lose with your bogey five."

JD turned away and approached one of the tournament officials who had been observing the match. Explaining what had just happened, he asked for a ruling. The official, who also happened to be a club member, looked at JD and asked, "Did anyone else observe this event?"

"Well, I don't think so. We were at the right-side bunker and all of the spectators were on the other side of the green."

Spreading his hands, the official responded, "Since no one, other than you, observed this incident, it is your word against Mr. Waldorf's and quite frankly, his family have been members here for three generations. We will certainly believe his version over someone like you. So, good day, young man." And with that, the official turned and walked away.

Shaking his head, JD walked to the scoring tent, posted his score of being one down, finishing runner-up and conceding the win to Perry Waldorf IV.

Not wanting to stay around after the winner and runner-up presentations were made, Patrick and JD drove to Ed

Doyle's home. Thanking Ed once more for his kindness and hospitality, they loaded the car and began the long drive home.

During the trip, Patrick asked, "What's bothering you, JD?"

"Grandpa, my opponent cheated. When I approached the tournament official, he basically said that it was my opinion and didn't matter. What really bothers me is Perry's attitude and his dishonesty, as well as the attitude of the tournament official."

"JD, I understand why you are upset. Maybe I have sheltered you too much, but you are going to meet people who are not always honest, especially when a tournament can be won or lost by a single shot. You did the right thing, JD, and I am proud of the way you handled the situation. I once read something that was written by a sports writer who lived in the early 1900s. He was a very honorable man. I think his name was Grantland Rice. Anyway, he wrote that, *'It's not whether you win or lose, but rather how you play the game.'* You play the game as it should be played, JD, and I couldn't be any more proud of you."

"Thank you, Grandpa, I appreciate that, but I really wanted to win that championship."

"I know, son. You will have other chances. You took your opponent to the wire. We both know you have been gifted with an ability that few have. Your time will come."

Chapter I
The Letter

The area was known as 'Upper Monroe Avenue.' A first-time visitor to Grand Rapids, Michigan, would expect to find a neighborhood of upscale houses, surrounded by lush yards of perfectly manicured green grass. This, however, was far from what a person would see on a drive north from the downtown business section. The houses had been built just after the Second World War to provide for the men returning from overseas and their families. The structures were small, placed on modest sized lots that could only provide for a one-stall garage located at the back of a narrow driveway.

It was mid-October, the sky was gray and an early snow had melted, leaving the area wet and a little chilly. JD, as his school friends called him, was sitting on the upper front porch step of his grandfather's modest, one-story, two-bedroom, bath-and-a-half house. It was the only home he had ever known. He was a very athletic looking teenager with broad shoulders, a narrow waist and long well-muscled arms and legs. JD had grown in the last year to a height of six feet, which was tall for a boy his age. With his sandy blonde hair and striking blue eyes, he stood out wherever he went. He was sitting on the step with that day's mail in his hands. Separating the envelopes, he noticed one in particular. It didn't look like the other envelopes, it was more formal. Looking at it closely, he noticed the logo in the upper left-hand corner and the fact that the return address was The Augusta National Golf Club, Augusta, Georgia.

He had been expecting this envelope and the letter it contained ever since he had finished runner-up in the U.S. Amateur Golf tournament, which had been held just that past summer, outside of Chicago, Illinois, at the Medinah Country Club. JD knew deep in his heart that he wanted to play in the Masters Tournament the following April, but didn't know how it would be financially possible to pay for the trip south.

Looking again at the front of the envelope, he had to smile at the formality of the address. It was addressed to Mr. John David Andrews. He had always been JD to his grandfather, grandmother, and his school friends. He never expected to be addressed as Mr. John David Andrews, but there it was on the face of the envelope. He knew he would have to have a discussion with his grandfather about the possibility of traveling to Georgia, the following spring, to play in the Masters Tournament. However, he also knew they were not wealthy, by any means, and a trip to Atlanta might be financially out of reach.

Opening the envelope, JD read the letter. This letter was the formal invitation to come to Atlanta, Georgia, and participate as one of the amateur players in the tournament. There was also a response card with a pre-stamped return envelope. What was exciting to JD was the fact that he was only 15 years old and wouldn't be 16 until the following

January, just over two months before the tournament was being held. While he was sitting there thinking of these things, he began to remember how this had all happened.

He didn't really remember his parents. When he was five years old, his grandfather told him of the accident and how his parents had been killed on the highway driving to Chicago for the first vacation they had taken since he had been born, three years earlier. He only knew his grandparents, Patrick and Paulette Davis. When he had asked his grandfather why their name was Davis and his was Andrews, it was then that his grandfather told him that they were the parents of his mother. When she had died in the auto accident, they were the only remaining living relatives and had taken John David into their home and raised him as their own son.

Not long after that conversation, Patrick noticed his grandson was very quiet and withdrawn. This was not his normal behavior and so Patrick, who played golf in his furniture factory league, decided to ask John David if he would like to hit balls across the street in Riverside Park. Riverside, a very large park, is owned by the city and maintained by the municipal workers who take great pride in keeping the park clean and orderly. Stretching the length of four city blocks along the Grand River, it offered ponds, wooded areas, and wide-open spaces that made it perfect for hitting a golf ball without interfering with any other park activities. This was the beginning of JD's interest in golf and he took to it with an intensity that surprised his grandfather. From that point on, it seemed that every time Patrick returned from work, he would find his grandson across the street, in the park, hitting golf balls. Realizing that JD had a genuine passion for knocking the ball around the park, Patrick decided to purchase a used set of Walter Hagen clubs from a friend at the golf course where his factory league played, after work, every Tuesday, during the summer months.

From the moment Patrick gave his grandson the full set of golf clubs with a light canvas carry-bag, he would often find him in the park, shooting at the targets that they had set out together at varying distances. These targets were nothing more than coffee cans filled with dirt, but at least they gave some structure to the hitting of balls.

This routine of after-school and summertime practice went on for a couple of years until one day a friend from his furniture factory golf league approached Patrick. This friend had listened to Patrick talk about his grandson and had stopped at Riverside Park to watch JD hit balls at his makeshift targets. After watching him swing the clubs, he approached Patrick during their next league night and told him about a golf instructor who happened to own a driving range not too far from where Patrick lived.

It was then that JD was introduced to a man by the name of Andy Van Lear. At this time, JD was only eight years old but his golf swing was remarkable. Andy recognized immediately that he was a natural and so he began instructing him, starting with the putter and working his way backward through the set of golf clubs until JD was proficient with each one. They developed a routine where JD would ride his bike home from school and wait for Mr. Van Lear to take him to the practice range.

This routine went on for a couple of summers, until Mr. Van Lear suggested to JD's grandfather that perhaps it would be good to take him to a couple of municipal courses to see how he could do. So the following Saturday Patrick and JD ventured out to Lincoln, a local municipal golf course, paid the fee and walking side-by-side played nine holes of golf.

JD shot par on the first nine holes that he had ever played. After the round of golf, he and his grandfather went into the clubhouse to sit down and have a glass of Coca-Cola. The general manager of the club, Bill Rosen, happened to be walking by and heard JD and Patrick talking about his round of golf. Realizing that Patrick's grandson was only ten years old, the general manager approached, "Patrick, good to see you. Can I join you?"

"Sure, Bill, this is my grandson, JD. We just finished playing the front nine and my grandson shot even par."

Sitting down, Bill looked at JD, then turned to Patrick and asked, "How is it that your grandson has learned to play so well?" After explaining about Mr. Van Lear and how he took JD under his wing and had been instructing him for the past two years, Bill, the general manager, offered to have JD help retrieve balls on the practice range for free rounds of golf.

Patrick and JD agreed to this and since the course was really only a bike ride from home, JD started going to the course just about every day.

It was toward the end of that summer that he entered his first tournament. It was a junior tournament sponsored by the furniture factory where his grandfather, Patrick, was employed. It was a two-day event, 18 holes each day, and JD won the tournament by six shots. Summer was ending and he had to go back to school. It was then that his grandfather starting thinking about his grandson playing in many tournaments on many different courses the following summer. It was also at this time that JD's grandmother, Paulette Davis, became seriously ill and died, leaving a tremendous void in not only his grandfather's heart, but in JD's life as well. Without his grandmother there to greet him after returning from school, Patrick arranged with his next-door neighbor, Mrs. Clara Nimitz, to fill in and have him stay with her until he could arrive home from work.

The following spring, JD's grandfather talked with Andy Van Lear and Bill, the general manager of Lincoln Golf Course, about how to enter JD in the junior golf tournaments held in western Michigan.

Once they had looked at the dates for tournaments on various municipal courses, a schedule was outlined for the summer months. This was the time when JD really started playing serious tournament golf. His progress was remarkable. He won more tournaments than he lost and he was more excited than ever about playing the game. There were times when his grandfather could not take him to a tournament that they had scheduled and it seemed that Andy Van Lear was more than willing to drive him. As JD sat thinking about these things and about how the summers seemed to go by so rapidly and how this past summer, he actually finished runner-up in the U.S. Amateur, his grandfather came walking up the sidewalk. Patrick Davis did not have the height or build of his grandson. JD had inherited his build from his father and his fair hair and complexion from his mother. Patrick stood around five feet eight and had salt and pepper hair. His most outstanding features were his kind face and gentle nature. He greeted JD with a bright warm smile and sat down next to him on the front porch step.

"How was school today?"

"School was just fine, Grandpa."

Patrick looked down and asked, "Have we received any interesting mail?" JD handed his grandfather the letter from the Augusta National Golf Club. After reading the letter, Patrick looked into JD's eyes. "Well, how would you feel about playing in another state on a golf course that you have never seen, nor had the opportunity to play?"

JD's response of "I would love it" didn't surprise Patrick. He knew full well that JD would jump at any chance to play in any tournament for the pure enjoyment of it and the chance to compete against other players.

"Well," Patrick said, "let's have dinner, sleep on it, and discuss the possibilities tomorrow."

The following day was a Saturday and, after breakfast, JD and his grandfather went across the street to Riverside Park and while they were walking along the riverbank, Patrick explained to him that he wouldn't be able to drive him to Augusta National for the tournament. However, he did say that there was a way he could get there, if he was willing to take a bus and travel alone. JD's response was yes he would and with that decision made, they decided to send in the response card accepting the invitation to play in the Masters Tournament.

Chapter II
The Winter Months

At the end of October, the Michigan weather turned cold with snow covering everything. Andy Van Lear arranged for JD to hit into a net at the junior college athletic building, located only three miles from his home.

After school and on weekends, he would head to the field house and hit balls into the net that Andy Van Lear had set up, specifically for him, to keep his golf muscles in shape over the months that he could not play outside. This was one of the big disadvantages of living in a northern climate with a limited golf season. Most golfers from the southern states could play year-round and keep their game sharp. But hitting into a net was better than not hitting at all and so this was the routine that he fell into for the months after October, and he knew that he would be hitting into the net well into the month of March.

Shortly after they had received acknowledgment from Augusta National that JD was registered to play in the tournament, he and his grandfather had a discussion about travel arrangements and where he would stay during his week in Georgia.

Patrick had done his research through a friend who worked in the sports department of the *Grand Rapids Press*, the local newspaper, and felt he had a way for his grandson to safely travel to Augusta, Georgia, and have a nice place to room while he was there.

Seated at the kitchen table, Patrick told his grandson about his plan to purchase a Greyhound bus ticket, provide him with some cash and traveler's checks, and have him stay at a youth hostel, which was located just a few blocks from Augusta National Golf Club's front gate.

It was shortly after this discussion that another letter from Augusta arrived. This was a follow-up letter again acknowledging that JD was registered to play in the tournament, which was to begin in early April. This letter contained a pair of admission tickets for all four days of the tournament to be used by family or friends. In addition, there was mention of a packet of information that would be sent sometime around the middle of February explaining the details of the tournament schedule as well as information about accommodations for the amateurs.

It was during this time that his grandfather was working overtime at the furniture factory. Patrick would often get home late and would seem to be very tired. Not wanting to burden him with any additional details, JD stuffed the letter with the admission tickets into his golf bag and promptly forgot about them. He continued going to the junior college field house after school and on weekends trying to keep his golf swing fluid and his body in shape for the upcoming tournament. He knew that if the weather broke in mid-March, he would be able to get outside but that was not always certain given the Michigan weather conditions.

The winter months seemed to drag by slowly for JD. The closer the calendar got to April, the more excited he became. The weather did break in mid-March and he was able to get out and play some rounds at the Lincoln Golf Club. Andy Van Lear worked with him as much as he could from mid-March to the first of April. On April 2, JD's grandfather gave him the round-trip Greyhound bus ticket to Atlanta, Georgia.

"JD, you are going to have to transfer bus lines once you arrive in Atlanta, to take you out to the youth hostel where you will be staying. As you know, I have been working a lot of overtime which covers your expenses. Here is an envelope with $100 in cash and $400 in American Express traveler's checks." Putting his arm around JD's shoulder, he told him that, "I will be able to take you to the Greyhound bus station and see you off on Friday. It is a long bus trip and will take about 24 hours with numerous stops along the way."

"I will be packed and ready to go. I know that you have been working overtime so that I could have this chance to play in Atlanta and I want you to know how much I appreciate it, Grandpa." He knew that the amount of money and the time that his grandfather had put into his game was no small sacrifice and he wanted his grandfather to know how much he appreciated everything.

After thanking his grandfather, JD phoned Andy Van Lear and thanked him for all that he had done.

"JD, it has been a privilege working with you. It is not often that I have the good luck to find someone who has the talent and a love for the game of golf that you do. I wish you the best of luck, but above all, enjoy your time at the tournament."

Placing the phone back on the receiver JD started to think about the upcoming trip and how much he was looking forward to playing in the Masters Tournament. He realized this was going to be an experience of a lifetime and was surprised that he was getting this opportunity at such a young age.

Double-checking his golf bag and suitcase, he was satisfied that everything was ready. Now all he had to do was wait for Friday morning when he and his grandfather would go to the Greyhound station, where he would say goodbye, board the bus, and travel south to the state of Georgia.

Chapter III
Bus Trip to Atlanta

After what seemed to be a very long time, short that it actually was, Friday, April 5th dawned bright and sunny. JD was ready. He actually did not sleep the entire night and his grandfather found him sitting at the kitchen table, dressed and ready to go. After a quick cup of coffee, Patrick helped him load his clubs and suitcase into the car and drove the six miles to the bus station.

Patrick double-checked with JD that he had the bus ticket, the money for his stay in Augusta, and the American Express traveler's checks. After he satisfied his grandfather that all was set, they embraced each other for a long couple of minutes. Finally, JD checked his bag and clubs, but just before boarding, his grandfather handed him a small, pocket-sized, flip-top notebook. "JD, I wish with all my heart that I could go to Augusta with you. Since that is not possible, I would like you to keep a journal of all that you experience from now until you arrive back in Grand Rapids. By doing this, I will be able to read it after you return home and then I will be able to somewhat live the trip with you, even if I cannot actually be there." With another brief hug, and a promise to keep the journal, JD boarded the Greyhound bus for the most exciting trip of his young life.

Once the other passengers found their seats, the door was closed and the silver bus with the image of a greyhound dog painted on both sides, pulled out of the station and turned toward US131 South, the highway leading out of Grand Rapids, Michigan. JD settled back and looking out of the window, watched as the city landscape turned into open countryside. He was excited, but tired, from lack of sleep and soon his eyes grew heavy and he dozed off into a dreamless rest.

The Greyhound bus, traveling south on Highway 131 took about an hour to reach I-94 going east. After a couple of hours, it was crossing into Ohio, finally hooking up to Highway I-75 toward Dayton, eventually passing through Kentucky, then crossing into Tennessee straight onto I-275 South, and then reaching I-640 East.

Once the bus was on I-640, it travelled to Asheville, North Carolina. This was the location of a major, southern, Greyhound Bus Terminal. For many passengers, this was their final destination and they left the bus, collected their travel bags and entered the terminal to greet their waiting family members. Watching the people pass through the double doors into the waiting area, JD noticed the most beautiful teenage girl that he had ever seen, standing off to the side, letting the people pass by. She stood out because of her height. He estimated she was almost as tall as he was. Her full head of thick blonde hair fell to her shoulders and when she looked up at the bus, the beauty of her face took his breath away. Not wanting to appear to be staring, JD looked away and busied himself with tidying up the area around him.

Shortly before the bus was to pull out of the terminal, she boarded and walked to where he was sitting. "Would you mind if I sit here?" she asked. Before he could respond, she sat in the seat next to him. Turning to face him, she said, "Hello, my name is Caroline, what's yours?"

Feeling his face get warm, he knew he was blushing, but he still had enough presence of mind to respond by extending his right hand to shake hers, and looking into her bright green eyes said, "My name is John David Andrews, but everyone calls me JD."

"Well, JD, where are you from and where are you going?"

The distance from Asheville to Atlanta, Georgia, is approximately 208 miles and takes about three and a half hours driving south on Highway I-85. From the moment Caroline said hello, JD was lost in conversation with this beautiful, energetic girl.

Looking into those captivating green eyes, JD said, "I'm from Grand Rapids, Michigan, and I am going to Atlanta to play in the Masters Tournament."

"Wow. Aren't you kind of young to be playing in such a famous event?"

After explaining how he qualified as an amateur and having received the invitation, JD asked her, "What were you doing in Asheville?"

With a smile that seemed to light up her entire face, Caroline said, "I was visiting my grandmother and grandfather. I really don't get to see them except on holidays and I wanted to spend a couple of weeks with just the three of us."

After these first few comments, the rest of the trip seemed to just fly by as JD and Caroline shared stories of family history and their mutual interest in sports.

While they were getting to know each other, the bus travelled south, eventually connecting with I-20 West toward Columbia/Augusta, then I-520 West toward North Augusta and finally, I-278 West crossing into Georgia. Approaching Augusta, the Greyhound took a turn onto the Broad Street ramp and proceeded to travel toward the downtown area. After a series of lane changes, the bus finally turned left onto 7th Street and pulled into the Augusta, Georgia Greyhound bus terminal.

The entire trip from Grand Rapids, Michigan, to Augusta, Georgia, was 890 miles and, with stops in various cities along the way, had taken 22 hours and 20 minutes.

Whenever the bus stopped, JD would get off, stretch his legs, use the available facilities, and purchase a sandwich and Coca-Cola to satisfy his hunger. He also took these short stops to write his impressions of the trip and his views of the countryside in the notebook that his grandfather had given him.

It was a long trip, but he was finally in Augusta, Georgia, home of the Masters Tournament! And, he reflected, he had met a very interesting, beautiful, young girl his own age along the way.

After they stepped off the bus, JD looked at Caroline and asked, "Where do you go from here?"

"Oh, my father is picking me up and we will go right home. How about you, do you need a ride?"

Not wishing to impose on her or her father, he just said, "Thanks, but I have made arrangements."

"Well then, JD, it was very nice meeting you and good luck in the tournament."

As she turned to walk toward the exit, JD found himself wishing she lived close to him back home so that he could really get to know her well.

After he had collected his clubs and suitcase, he approached the desk clerk for directions to a local bus that could take him to the youth hostel where his grandfather had reserved a room for the week.

The clerk responded by telling him to, "Cross the street and wait at the covered bench near the corner and take bus #7, and let the driver know where you have to go."

It was Saturday, April 6th, and JD was anxious to check into his room.

After waiting about 30 minutes, bus #7 stopped and the driver waited while JD loaded his suitcase and clubs, paid the fare, and settled into a seat directly across from him. Noticing the clubs, the driver looked at him and asked, "Where are you going?"

"I would like to go to the youth hostel located at 3010 Washington Road."

"Well, get comfortable and I will drop you off just a couple of blocks away."

Looking at JD's golf bag, he asked, "Are you going to play in the tournament?"

"Yes, I am."

"If you don't mind my asking, how can someone so young be playing in such an important event?"

"I am young, but I received an invitation to play as a result of finishing as the runner-up in last year's U.S. Amateur Event in Chicago, Illinois."

After a few moments of silence, the bus stopped to let the only other passenger off. Instead of immediately driving off, the driver turned and asked, "What is your name?"

Responding by extending his hand, he looked the driver directly in the eyes and said, "John David Andrews, but everyone back home calls me JD."

Smiling, the driver then introduced himself as Herman Eldman. JD couldn't help but notice how dark Herman's skin was and how white was his hair. It was a striking contrast but he kept this observation to himself. To fill the silence that followed, they started talking about the tournament.

As the bus travelled on, Herman mentioned, "It has always been my dream to take my son to the Masters Tournament, even if it was just for the practice round."

When JD asked why he had never done it, Herman laughed and said, "I really couldn't afford the tickets on the wages that I make as a bus driver."

Then, just when Herman stopped the bus to let him off, JD remembered the letter with the two tickets that he had put into his golf bag. Asking Herman to wait while he removed the suitcase and golf bag from the bus, he zipped open the side pocket and took out the envelope that contained the letter and the tickets. Removing the tickets, he handed them to Herman.

"Please use these for yourself and your son."

At first, Herman refused to accept them, but when JD explained that he had no one with him and wouldn't need them, he gratefully accepted the tickets and said that he and his son would look for JD on the course, during the tournament. With that, Herman directed him to turn left and walk two blocks to the youth hostel. JD thanked him and told him he hoped to see him at the tournament. After closing the bus door, Herman noticed that the two tickets he had been given covered admittance to all four days of the tournament. He knew then that he would be taking some days off during the coming week, as would his son, so that they could be together for the Masters Tournament, a dream come true, as unlikely as it seemed.

Chapter IV
Youth Hostel

As the bus pulled away, JD with his suitcase in one hand and his golf bag over his shoulder, walked the two blocks to the youth hostel and checked in. The room was not particularly large but when he tested the bed, he found that it was quite comfortable. He always did like a good night's sleep before a tournament and with a comfortable bed, he felt he would be in good shape.

Once he put his clothes in the four-drawer dresser, showered and put on a fresh shirt and pair of slacks, he walked out the front door, crossed Washington Road and found a diner that had a bright red neon 'Open' sign in the front window. Upon entering, he was greeted with a friendly, "Hello, take a seat and I will be with you in a minute." Looking to his left, he saw the person who had greeted him with such a friendly voice. He found that he was looking at a striking woman that he guessed, was about in her mid-forties. Her hair was an auburn red and her skin was a very pale white. But most striking were her large hazel eyes. Not wanting to stare, he looked away and took a seat at the nearest vacant booth. After a satisfying meal of roast beef, mashed potatoes with gravy, and some southern biscuits covered in melted butter, he returned to the hostel for what he hoped would be a solid night's sleep.

Before turning in, he took his journal and spent the next fifteen minutes writing about the bus ride from the Greyhound terminal. He also described his encounter with Herman Eldman, the local bus driver, and how he gave him the Masters Tournament admittance tickets, so that he and his son could enjoy being spectators. JD also described the diner and the friendly waitress who served him his first southern meal. Writing about meeting Caroline and how much he enjoyed being with her on the bus ride from Asheville, NC, to Atlanta, Georgia, he found that he was smiling and felt that his grandfather would like her very much, should they ever have a chance to meet.

Setting aside the journal, he walked over to a small corner table that had a lamp and a black, desktop, rotary dial phone. Picking up the receiver he dialed 0 for the operator and asked to place a collect call. Once the connection was made, JD and his grandfather spent the next ten minutes talking about his trip south, the comfort of his room, and was all okay? Assuring his grandfather that all was well, he promised to call each evening before going to bed.

After saying goodbye, JD hung up the phone and spent the next few minutes getting ready for bed.

At first he could only lay there with thoughts drifting through his head as to what might happen during the tournament. His primary concern was playing in an event of such stature as the Masters with absolutely no knowledge of the golf course layout. The one nagging thought that kept repeating in his head, over and over, was how he could possibly gain enough experience in just the practice rounds, that would be held on Monday, Tuesday and Wednesday, to carry him through the event or at least give himself enough experience to make a decent showing for the first two rounds on Thursday and Friday.

Finally, the exhaustion from the long bus trip took its toll and he drifted off into a deep, restful sleep.

Chapter V
Augusta National

It was early, Sunday morning, April 7, 1958, when JD opened his eyes with the sudden realization that his week at the Masters was about to begin. Checking the alarm clock that his grandfather had put into his luggage, he noted that it was 5:30 a.m., pre-dawn in Augusta, Georgia. Placing his bare feet on the floor, he stretched and realized he was much too excited to stay in bed. Crossing to the bathroom, he brushed his teeth and took a quick shower before dressing in a light-colored golf shirt and a cream-colored pair of golf slacks. Slipping on his street shoes, he grabbed his golf bag and golf cap, and proceeded to exit the hostel. Once outside, he took a deep breath, inhaling the sweet southern air and started walking the four blocks down Washington Road to the front gate of the Augusta National Golf Club. As he was walking, JD took in the sights of the surrounding neighborhood. To his right he passed what could only be described as a commercial area. However, in between the business buildings, there was an occasional house that reminded him of the modest homes from his neighborhood back in Grand Rapids, Michigan. Being as early as it was, no one was up and his walk to the golf course was a quiet, short journey.

The gates to the club were closed and locked. JD had thoughts of sitting to the side on the well-manicured grass and waiting for someone to open the gates. However, walking to his right, he noticed a slight gap between the brick column that the gate was bolted to and the well-manicured hedge that seemed to block the view of the interior area. Without much thought, he slipped through the narrow opening and started walking up Magnolia Lane toward the front entrance of the magnificent clubhouse. Never in his short life had he ever seen anything so beautiful as the trees, flowers, and expertly manicured lawn. The trees actually formed a canopy over the road that made it seem like he was walking through a tunnel. Lining each side of the gray road surface were green colored bricks. Looking through the tunnel of trees, he could see a Masters logo made up of yellow flowers adorning a grassy knoll and a green and white canvas awning that was directly over the front entrance. A beautiful white railing with vertical slats stretched above, bordering a balcony stretching across the second floor. The beauty of the clubhouse and surrounding grounds was absolutely stunning.

Once he had arrived at the steps leading to the front door of the clubhouse, he realized that no one was around. So, taking his invitation letter out of his golf bag, he took a seat on a lower step, just off to the right, and waited for someone to show up. After what seemed to be an hour, JD was guessing it was about 7 a.m., a gentleman opened the front clubhouse door, walked down the steps and asked, "Young man, who are you and why are you sitting on the front steps of the Augusta National Golf Club?"

JD, standing and facing this impeccably dressed gentleman, introduced himself. "I'm John David Andrews." He then offered him the letter that was his invitation to play in the Masters Tournament. After reading the letter, the gentleman facing him extended his hand and, with a warm smile, introduced himself as Mr. Harold B. Wilkinson III, the Augusta National Club Chairman.

"Well, Mr. Andrews, why don't you leave your clubs on the porch and come inside with me?" Opening the door, he asked, "Have you eaten breakfast?"

"No, sir, I was too excited to stop and eat."

"Well then, Mr. Andrews, would you like to join me for some eggs and sausage in the breakfast room? I have to attend to a few early morning business matters, but then we can enjoy a quiet breakfast and get to know each other. Why don't you take a seat in the side Reading Room and make yourself at home?"

"Thank you, Mr. Wilkinson, for your kindness."

"Not at all, Mr. Andrews, I'm looking forward to getting to know you. I should be back in about an hour, so please make yourself at home, until I return."

Chapter VI
Reading Room

When JD was alone, he looked around the Reading Room. The room was very warm and inviting with three very rich looking tables, each having four captain's chairs. There was a fireplace on the far wall with bookshelves, encased with small glass doors, on both sides. The carpeting was a deep green color and against the wall was a writing desk with a green leather inlaid top.

When he had left Grand Rapids, his grandfather had given him a small spiral bound notebook that flipped open, top to bottom. He had suggested that keeping a journal of his experiences in Augusta would be a good thing to do.

JD did have the notebook in his back pocket but he needed a pen or pencil. Sitting at the desk, he opened the top center drawer but did not find either. Opening the upper right drawer, he did find a writing pen and reaching for it, his hand bumped a small, note page sized, spiral notebook. Removing it from the drawer, JD read the handwritten title on the front cover. He inhaled a sharp breath as he read 'How I Play the Course' by Bobby Jones.

Chapter VII
The Notebook

Opening the notebook, JD realized that this could help him understand the golf course and make up for the fact that he had never played Augusta National.

Taking his own notebook and turning it over so that he could make notes from the back page forward, leaving the front pages for his journal entries, he started to read the Bobby Jones notebook and began making notes in his. The notebook started with hole #1 and proceeded through all 18 holes, with short comments on what club he played, and from what area, on each hole. When he had finished making his own notes, he noticed, by the grandfather clock positioned in the far corner of the room, that 45 minutes had passed. Opening the drawer, he replaced the Bobby Jones notebook and pen while returning his flip notebook to his own back pocket. Standing, he stretched his legs and walked over to the bookshelves to look at what books were there. Just then Mr. Wilkinson returned and asked JD to join him for breakfast. As they walked into the dining room, JD noticed how plush everything seemed and was impressed with the richness of the clubhouse interior.

Chapter VIII
Breakfast

The dining room, while not elaborately over-the-top in elegance, was certainly very comfortable. White tablecloths covered each table and a setting for two had been arranged.

After being seated, Mr. Wilkinson was served coffee and water was offered to JD. Sipping his coffee, Mr. Wilkinson looked at JD, smiled and asked, "How is it that you have arrived so early at the front steps of the Augusta National Golf Club?" As JD was about to explain the trip south, the youth hostel, and walking over to the golf club, Mr. Wilkinson looked up to find his assistant, Charles Wareng, standing just over his right shoulder. Leaning down, Charles whispered something to Mr. Wilkinson, placed a note in front of him, and took a step back. After reading the note, Mr. Wilkinson looked at his guest, "Young man, I must apologize. I have to attend to a situation that has occurred with the tournament scheduling of on-site vendors. Charles, would you see that Mr. Andrews enjoys his breakfast and offer him any help he needs to get settled?"

"I most certainly will, Mr. Wilkinson."

"Thank you and I look forward to having an uninterrupted visit with you soon, Mr. Andrews."

Excusing himself, he then left to take care of the vendor situation.

Charles sat down as the server cleared the area where Mr. Wilkinson had been sitting and asked JD, "What can I do to help you get settled?" After answering his questions about where to find times for practice rounds and where to store his clubs, locker room admittance, and other useful golfer questions, JD and Charles settled in to enjoy a breakfast of hotcakes, scrambled eggs, toast, and a southern staple that JD learned was called grits. Most of the casual conversation between Charles and JD revolved around the history of Augusta National and the Masters Tournament. Once they had finished breakfast, Charles asked, "Is there anything else I can help you with?"

"Would it be okay to walk the course, without golf clubs, just to take it all in and get a sense of the layout?"

"Certainly, take your clubs to the storage attendant (directing him where to go) and have him show you where the locker room is and which locker to use for the tournament. Once those details have been attended to, you certainly can walk the course and I hope you enjoy the rest of the day."

JD shook Charles's hand, "Thank you for your help and please thank Mr. Wilkinson for his kind greeting and hospitality."

Once Charles had left, JD retrieved his clubs, found the attendant and introducing himself as JD Andrews, explained what he needed. In return, he was welcomed warmly by the friendliest, most soft-spoken black man he had ever met.

Looking at JD with his soft brown eyes, he smiled widely. "Could you please repeat your name for me?" When JD told him to just call him by his initials, he responded, "I certainly cannot do that. What is your full name?"

"Well, sir, what is your name?"

"I, young man, have been blessed with a true southern name. I am Emery Abraham Lincoln Smith, but you can just call me Emery."

"I am very pleased to meet you, Emery. My full name is John David Andrews."

Emery, giving him another big, bright, friendly smile, reached out his hand and shaking JD's, he took his clubs. "It is a pleasure to meet you, Mr. Andrews. During your stay here at Augusta National, I and the rest of the staff will be using your proper name."

JD suddenly realized, that here in the South, things were different and he would just have to accept the more formal traditions.

After storing his clubs, Emery introduced JD to James Henry, the locker room attendant. James greeted him with the same formality as Emery, with a bright smile, a friendly manner, and proceeded to show him which locker he could use during the tournament. James then gave him a quick tour of the full locker room, showers, and facilities. Once he was satisfied that JD was comfortable with the locker room area, he excused himself and left him standing in front of the locker he was supposed to use while at the Masters Tournament.

Returning to the club storage area, he asked Emery if he could get his golf shoes out of the side pocket of his bag. Changing shoes, he put his soft-soled street shoes in the bag and slipped on the golf shoes. Having only one pair of golf shoes, he didn't really see a need to use a locker. He felt he would just wear his golf clothes to the club each day and change his shoes, like he had just done.

Thanking Emery for his kindness, he set out to walk the grounds. Watching him walk off, Emery thought to himself that Mr. Andrews was awfully young to be here alone. With that thought, Emery watched as JD passed the corner of the clubhouse and walked toward the first tee.

For the next three-and-a-half hours, JD walked each hole of the Augusta National Course and was stunned at the beauty and absolute perfect conditioning of the grounds. Pausing on each tee box, he took out his flip top notebook, which happened to fit perfectly in his back right pants pocket, and reviewed the notes he had copied from Bobby Jones's booklet. After spending the late morning and on into the early afternoon, walking the course, he returned to the club storage area, switched shoes, and asked Emery if he might have a schedule sheet for the next three days of practice rounds. Without thinking much about it, Emery handed him a sheet of paper that outlined the events and times. Thanking him, JD walked down Magnolia Lane, out the front gate, and returned to his room at the youth hostel. Being tired from his first day at Augusta, he stretched out on his bed and promptly fell into a deep satisfying sleep.

Upon waking, he was surprised to find that it was 6:30 p.m. Being hungry, he walked to the diner and had a full meal of pork chops with mashed potatoes, green beans and of course, grits, which, with a lot of butter, pepper, and salt, he was beginning to like. After the meal, he walked around the area, eventually working his way back to his room. Once he had showered, laid out his clothes for his Monday practice round, he took the journal notebook and wrote down his thoughts about all that he had experienced during his second day in Augusta. He took great care to record how kind he had found everyone, especially Mr. Wilkinson, his assistant, Charles, and Emery, the bag room attendant. Setting aside the journal, JD used the phone on the small corner table and placed a collect call to his grandfather.

JD and his grandfather talked for thirty minutes with JD relating all that had happened that day. Eventually, his grandfather thanked him for calling and asked him to call each night about the same time. "I love you, JD, and wish you the best of luck in the coming days."

"Thanks, Grandpa, I love you too and wish you were here with me." Hanging up, JD experienced a strong sense of homesickness, missing his grandfather and their warm, familiar house. However, once he began to think about the Monday practice round, he settled down and fell asleep thinking about playing in a golf tournament, on a golf course like none other he had ever seen.

Chapter IX
Monday Practice Round

Monday of tournament week was a beautiful, cloudless day. JD awoke at 6:00 a.m., dressed in his golf clothes, and walked to the diner. After seating himself in a booth just inside the front door, he was greeted with the same friendly 'hello' that he had been greeted with on his first visit. Looking up, he was again staring into the large, hazel eyes of the waitress that had served him his evening meal that previous Saturday. Responding with his own 'hello,' he noticed that the name tag on the server's blouse read Liz and added that to his greeting.

Smiling, Liz said, "Well, if you are going to be a regular customer, I should know your name."

"My name is JD."

"Really, what does JD stand for?"

"My full name is John David Andrews, but everyone knows me by JD."

"JD it is then and what would you like for breakfast?"

After ordering, he sat quietly, thinking about the day ahead. Once the food arrived, he enjoyed a full, very filling, breakfast of eggs over easy, toast, a full stack of hotcakes, sausage, and grits. After paying his bill, he smiled at Liz, "Thank you for the good service."

"You're more than welcome, young man, please visit us again."

"I will be here for the week, so I think I will be back."

"So, I have to ask, where are you from and what brings you to our fair state for just one week?"

JD explained, "I am a golfer from Grand Rapids, Michigan, and I am going to play in the Masters Tournament."

"You must be a pretty good golfer to play in that tournament."

"I am a pretty good golfer, at least good enough to be invited to play, but I will have to see how it goes this week."

"Well, I work most mornings, so I will be here to serve you breakfast."

"Great, sounds good to me," and with a nod toward Liz, he left the diner and enjoyed his walk to the front gate of Augusta National.

Arriving at 7:30 a.m., he presented his letter of invitation to the guard. Looking at JD, the guard was skeptical that someone so young and arriving alone could actually be a participant in a tournament of such stature. Asking him to wait a minute, he entered the narrow guardhouse just to the left of the main entrance and called the clubhouse. Being assured that John David Andrews was indeed one of the amateur players, the guard gave JD a player's pass, telling him, "Keep this with you and show it to anyone who might question your being on the grounds." Wishing him luck, he made a welcoming hand gesture toward Magnolia Lane.

Walking toward the large white clubhouse and looking at the beautiful flowers, magnolia trees, and the perfectly groomed grounds, he was again struck by the total magnificence of his surroundings. Arriving at the end of Magnolia Lane, he walked around the right side of the clubhouse, to the bag storage area. Greeting Emery, the club storage attendant, he asked for his golf bag, telling Emery he was going to get in a practice round.

"Well, the practice rounds don't begin until 8:30 this morning. However, since you're already here, I'll get your clubs and you can ask Joe, our head groundskeeper, if he will let you go early."

Shouldering his bag, he said, "Thanks, Emery," and turned to walk to the first tee. Once there, he sat down, took his golf shoes out of the side pocket of the bag, put them on and put his street shoes in the bag. Getting up he noticed the groundskeeper near the first tee. Approaching, JD said, "Hello."

The groundskeeper responded with, "Hello, son, can I help you?"

"Yes, I wonder if I might tee off a little early for my first practice round. I'm alone and won't get in anyone's way."

"Well, it's okay with me, the crews are finished prepping the course so you won't be bothering anyone. But, just to be sure, check with our starter. He is just over there by the first tee, getting ready for the practice rounds to begin."

"Thanks," said JD and walked over to the starter.

Looking up, the starter was surprised to see a young boy with clubs over his shoulder walking toward him. "Can I help you, son?"

"Yes, my name is JD Andrews and I will be playing as an amateur in the tournament. I was wondering if I could get in an early practice round, alone, since I'm really not here with anyone?"

Although somewhat surprised, the starter said, "Sure, my name is John and you go right ahead." With that short introduction, John turned and walked over to the groundskeeper to discuss the course conditions and that day's practice rounds.

It was now 8:00 a.m. and JD was still the only player around. Setting his bag down and pulling his golf glove on, he took a ball and tee, and prepared to hit his first shot at the Augusta National Golf Club.

Reaching into his back pocket, he took out his notebook and read about how Bobby Jones would play hole #1. He realized that he should really play different shots from different spots on each hole. Taking a couple more balls from his bag, he was ready to go.

Referring to his notes he read: *Hole #1, named 'Tea Olive,' 400 yards, must hit a long straight tee shot. Setting up a good second shot, go for the middle of the green.* With that short review, he put his tee in the ground, placed his ball on top, and hit his drive solidly down the middle of the fairway. Picking up his bag, he replaced his driver, shouldered the bag, and walked down the middle of the fairway to where his ball had stopped rolling.

Reaching his ball, he again reviewed his notes. Bobby Jones had written, *for the second shot, always go for the center of the green, setting up a possible birdie putt.*

JD, having hit his drive close to 290 yards, had just a short 110-yard wedge shot, slightly uphill to the green. Replacing the notebook into his back pocket, he selected his wedge and hit it square and clean with the ball landing on the green, slightly left of center. He then tossed two additional balls onto the ground, one about twenty yards to the left and the other about thirty yards to the right and hit those towards the green. After a few putts to get used to various areas of the green, he picked up his golf balls, shouldered his bag, and walked to the second tee.

Repeating the method he used for the first hole and referring to his Bobby Jones's 'How I Play the Course' notes, JD proceeded to play 2-3 shots at various positions on each of the next 8 holes, trying to perform like the notebook had it laid out.

On holes #10 through #18, he repeated the process and finished just as the first of the professionals began making the turn to the 10th tee.

With his first practice round finished, he decided to carry his bag back to his room. Changing into his street shoes and placing his golf shoes back into his bag, he shouldered the light carry bag and without looking back, walked down Magnolia Lane, out through the front entrance and proceeded, unobserved, to make the walk back to the youth hostel. Sitting on the edge of his bed, he took a wet towel, cleaned his clubs and shoes. Storing them in a corner and closing the door to his room, JD walked the couple of blocks to the café where he had been eating his meals.

While enjoying a burger, fries, and a strawberry milkshake, he went over, in his mind, each shot of his practice round. He realized that although he had only played the course once, that by referring to his Bobby Jones notes, before each shot, including putts, he was able to play a very good round of golf. Finishing his food, he paid the restaurant check and asked for directions to the nearest movie theatre.

Walking the six blocks to the movie house, he purchased a ticket and settled in for the 2½ hour *From Earth to the Moon* movie, a science fiction film that took his mind completely off golf. When the movie was over, he walked back to his room and took a nice long nap.

Waking to the twilight of early evening, he walked back to the café and had a dinner of meatloaf, mashed potatoes, milk and apple pie for dessert. With his hunger satisfied, he returned to his room and spent the next half hour writing in his journal about the day, his practice round and how accurate he had found the Bobby Jones notes about how to play the course. Setting aside his notebook, he walked to the small table and again made a collect call to Grand Rapids. Talking to his grandfather seemed to have a calming effect on his emotions and he was very thankful to have such a solid, well-grounded connection to home.

Once he and his grandfather had said their goodbyes, JD washed his face, brushed his teeth, changed into his night clothes, and crawled into bed. Sleep didn't take long and he was out by 10:30 p.m.

Chapter X
Tuesday Practice Round

When the alarm clock went off, JD had already been awake for over an hour. While still in bed, he had been mentally reviewing the Monday morning practice round. Going over each hole, he was trying to decide if he should have played any shot differently than he did.

Once the alarm rang, he decided to just trust the notes that he had written from Bobby Jones's notebook and try to put the best golf swing he possibly could on the ball and be satisfied with that.

Following the routine that he had established since arriving in Augusta, Georgia, he washed, dressed and walked to the local café where he had pretty much eaten every meal. Once again, he was greeted with a cheerful 'hello' from Liz, the waitress that had served him his breakfast the day before. Only this time she added 'JD' to the hello.

Smiling, he responded with a friendly, "Good morning, Liz."

"And what will you be ordering today, young man?"

"Well, I think I will go with scrambled eggs, ham, toast, and of course, grits," he responded.

"Sounds good," said Liz and she walked to the kitchen to put in his order.

After finishing his breakfast, he paid his check and thanked Liz for being so friendly to an out-of-towner.

"It's nice to see a new face once in a while, hope to see you again," she said.

Feeling satisfied after eating a hearty breakfast, he returned to his room. Once there, he used the bathroom, picked up his golf bag, and walked the few short blocks to the front gate of the Augusta National Golf Club. The time was 7:35 a.m. walking through the front gate, JD went straight to the first tee and just like the first day, he found no one waiting to play. Having been given the go ahead on Monday, he figured no one would object if he chose to practice early again. He sat at the first tee, slipped off his street shoes, reached into the side pocket of the golf bag and took out his golf shoes. Once he had them laced securely, he put his street shoes into the bag, stood up, stretched a bit, and was ready to go.

Selecting his driver, he again took out his notebook and reread the notes he had written about playing hole #1. *Must hit a long straight tee shot*, he had written, *setting up a good second shot, go for the middle of the green.* Sliding his notebook into his back pocket, he hit the first shot of his second practice round. Once again, he was by himself. No one seemed to mind and JD, just like at home, didn't mind playing alone.

Referring to his notes, he played each hole as if he was playing in the tournament, with the exception that he would putt from different parts of each green to get some sense of how the balls would break, should the pin placements be in tough-to-reach areas.

After finishing his second eighteen holes, he was satisfied that by utilizing the notebook as a guide, he could at least play Augusta National with some confidence. Switching out of his golf shoes and into his street shoes, he shouldered his bag for the walk past the front gate and back to his room to shower and visit the café for lunch.

After lunch, he took in another movie, returned to his room and like the previous afternoon, took a good long nap.

Once awake, he made an early phone call to his grandfather, answering all of the questions about the golf course, his game, and how he was feeling physically.

He told his grandfather he loved him and hearing the same, said goodbye and hung up the phone. JD sat for a while, missing having his grandfather close by his side. He realized that when he was not on the golf course, he was definitely more than a little homesick.

Once the feeling subsided, he left his room, went out the front door, and walked a while. Eventually, he arrived at the diner. After finishing a satisfying supper, he returned to his room, wrote in his journal about the day's events, and turned in for the night.

Chapter XI
Wednesday Practice Round

Getting out of bed at 6 a.m., JD dressed in his golf clothes and made his way to what had become his favorite diner. Sitting in a booth, he looked up and once again, he was looking into the eyes of the woman that had greeted him every day when he had arrived for breakfast.

"Good morning, JD."

Her smile was infectious and he responded with a bright smile of his own and a friendly, "Good morning, Liz." Since this was his third consecutive breakfast at the same diner, he smiled and said, "What would you recommend I have for breakfast today?"

"Today is Wednesday, JD, and we have a mid-week special of three eggs over easy, bacon, sausage patties and grits."

"Sounds perfect, let's go with that."

When the food arrived, JD smiled and thanked her for the quick service. After finishing the rather large and satisfying breakfast, he paid his bill and said, "I will see you tomorrow, same time, same booth."

As he walked out, Liz smiled and said, "OK, see you tomorrow."

JD returned to his room, picked up his golf bag, and headed for Augusta National.

Walking up to the front gate entrance, he stopped and asked the guard his name.

"My name is Phil and what is yours, young man?"

"John David Andrews," he replied, "but you can just call me JD."

Since this was the second time they had met, with JD arriving so early, Phil just waved his hand and told him to "Have a nice day!" With that greeting, JD began walking up Magnolia Lane and was once again struck by the overwhelming beauty of the lush surroundings.

Walking to the club storage area, he spotted Emery and with a bright smile on his face he greeted him with a, "Good morning, Emery, it looks like another beautiful day here in Augusta."

"Well, Mr. Andrews, it certainly does, what can I do for you on this fine southern morning?"

JD smiled again at the formality of being addressed as Mr. Andrews and asked Emery if he would take his clubs, also mentioning that his golf shoes were in the golf bag side pocket. "After I'm finished with my round, I would like to keep them here." Then, remembering his manners added, "If that is okay with you, Emery?"

"Why yes, Mr. Andrews, it is fine with me and if you need anything else, just ask." Thanking Emery, JD reached into his bag and took out six brand new Titleist golf balls. He then removed his golf shoes from the bag. After putting them on, he placed his street shoes into the side pocket.

When he started to turn away, Emery asked, "Aren't you going to take your clubs for your practice round?"

"No, just these balls to see how the greens roll."

Emery was surprised but didn't say anything as he watched him walk toward the first tee.

Once again, he was early and no one was around to ask what he was doing. So, JD walked off the first tee and wandered down the first hole like a spectator. Referring to his notebook, he refreshed his memory about how he played each shot, tee-to-green, the first two days. Once he reached the green on Hole #1, he reached into his pockets and took out the balls. Taking three in each hand, he started walking around the green, counterclockwise, and dropped one ball at a time, at six-foot intervals. As each one would roll on the green, he would make a note about its direction and speed in his notebook. He did this because at the back of the Bobby Jones notebook, there was a section that discussed how the greens rolled and how tricky and fast they are. He decided to heed that advice and felt that if he rolled at least six balls on each green, from different areas, he could get a good idea of what Mr. Jones meant.

After walking all eighteen holes, referring to his notes on how to play each one and making new notes about how the balls rolled on each green, he was satisfied that he had prepared as much as he could.

Returning to the club storage area, he found Emery busy with the professionals, as he had to make sure they received the service and attention only Augusta National could provide with such perfection. Taking care of the golfers one after another, Emery did not notice JD standing off to the side. During a break in the seemingly endless stream of players, Emery looked up and noticed him.

"Well, young man, are you finished with your rather unique practice round?"

"Yes I am. Could I put these balls in my bag?"

"Sure thing," said Emery.

Bringing his bag, Emery looked at him and asked, "Do you know what your starting time is for the first round?"

"No, I don't. Could you find out for me?"

"Sure," said Emery. Taking a note pad, he wrote down the club storage room phone number and handing it to JD said, "Call at 4:30 p.m. and ask for me. I will be here and I will have all of the starting times. I have to make sure I have everyone's clubs ready at least two hours before they tee-off. So, you just call and I will let you know."

"Thanks, Emery, I will be sure to call somewhere around 4:30. Thank you so much."

Leaving the club storage area, JD wandered around like a visiting spectator. Getting hungry, he wandered to a concession area where he noticed people purchasing sandwiches and drinks. Deciding to try a pimento cheese sandwich and Coca-Cola, he discovered a rare treat in how good the sandwich was and how little it cost. Right then and there, he knew that this would be his lunch spot for the rest of the tournament.

Soon, there was a buzz going through the crowd and when JD asked what it was all about, he was told about the Par 3 contest. So, following the crowd he watched the professionals attempt to outdo each other. At the conclusion of the Par 3 contest, he noticed that time had slipped by and it was now twenty minutes past four. Walking to the bag storage area, he found Emery and asked if he had his tee time for the following morning.

"I do," said Emery, "It looks like you are the first time at 8:20 a.m. I will have your clubs ready at 6:30 so that you can loosen up on the practice range and spend some time on our putting green before you tee-off."

"Thanks, Emery. Does it say who I will be playing with?"

"Well, it just says you will be playing with a member of the club who will be acting as a marker. Someone must have withdrawn from the tournament and we now have an odd number of players, so you have to play with a fill-in."

"Well, okay, I will be here before 7 a.m. to warm up and get ready to start the round."

Shaking Emery's hand and thanking him for his help, he turned and walked toward the front drive that would lead him out of the gate and back to his room. Watching him leave, Emery thought about how unusual it was that a young player, like Mr. Andrews, seemed to be so alone that he needed to find out about his tee-time from the club storage attendant.

"Oh well," Emery said out loud and put the thought out of his mind.

After arriving at his room, JD showered, dressed, and walked to the café diner. He decided to order the daily special of pork BBQ with mashed potatoes, gravy, and a soft dinner roll. He ate his evening meal, quietly thinking about the next few days and wondering how much his notes would help during America's number one tournament, 'The Masters.'

Returning to the youth hostel, he decided to watch some TV in the community room. After a couple of hours, he went to his room, made his journal entries, phoned his grandfather, and decided to go to bed. Noticing it was 10 p.m., he crawled into bed and fell into a restless sleep.

Chapter XII
Day One, The Tournament

Waking at 5:30 a.m., JD dressed in his golf clothes, washed his face, and stepped outside the front door of the youth hostel. Already, he could tell the weather would provide great golf conditions. The weather forecast had said the tournament would enjoy the nicest stretch of weather that could ever be remembered for the playing of this major event.

Making his way to the diner for breakfast, he was in good spirits. Entering with his usual, "Good morning, Liz," he sat in what had become his favorite booth, just inside the front door.

"What would you like for breakfast today, JD?"

Smiling, because of the friendliness that he and Liz had come to share, he answered, "Let's go with two eggs over easy, wheat toast, bacon, sausage, and grits."

After writing his order on her pad, Liz looked at him and asked, "Do you have a big day ahead?"

"I do and I am going to need all the energy a full breakfast can provide."

"Well, this order should be just the ticket."

The food arrived and after finishing his very satisfying meal, he paid his check and as he approached the front door, he heard Liz wish him, "Good luck today."

"Thanks," he responded and opening the door he walked into the pleasure of a perfect Georgia morning.

As he approached the Augusta National front gate, the morning guard greeted him with a big smile, saying, "Hello, Mr. Andrews, I wish you a very pleasant round of golf today."

"Thank you, Phil, I appreciate that."

Turning, he walked up Magnolia Lane. Approaching the end of the lane, he turned toward the right corner of the clubhouse, making his way to the club storage area.

Emery greeted him with a friendly handshake and handed him his golf bag. He knew that Emery would have his bag ready since he was first off with the 8:20 a.m. starting time.

"Thanks, Emery, mind if I sit and put on my golf shoes?"

"Not at all, Mr. Andrews, and if you leave your street shoes, I will clean them for you."

JD smiled, "Thank you, Emery."

Lacing up his golf shoes, he handed his street shoes to Emery.

Shouldering his bag, he walked to the practice range. Setting his bag down, he noticed a man hitting range balls just a couple of club lengths away. JD said 'hello' and introduced himself.

"Pleased to meet you, Mr. Andrews, I am Harold Stone, a member here at Augusta National. I will be playing with you this morning as a marker. It seems we have had a withdrawal of one of our contestants, so I was asked to fill in."

"Well," said JD, "I am looking forward to our round."

"As am I," said Harold.

With the introductions completed, each man turned to the task of hitting the shots that would help loosen the golf muscles and get them ready for the 18 holes to follow.

After a half-hour of hitting practice shots, JD proceeded to the putting area and finished his preparation by putting a number of balls, from varying distances. When he was satisfied that his putting stroke was steady and ready, he returned the putter to his bag.

Picking up the bag, he started for the first tee. The time was 7:45 a.m. As he walked to the area near the right side of the first tee, he noticed Mr. Herman Eldman, the local bus driver, that he had given his tournament passes to, standing just outside the roped area with a younger man by his side. Walking over, he extended his hand with a big smile on his face.

"Hello, Mr. Eldman, I'm happy you could be here."

"Oh, so am I, JD, I mean Mr. Andrews."

"Well, between you and me, let's just go with JD."

"Okay, JD. I want to introduce you to my son, Joseph."

Shaking Joseph's hand, JD thanked him for being there with his dad.

"Oh, it's my treat, really," responded Joseph.

As JD was about to turn away, the starter for the tournament approached him.

"Excuse me, Mr. Andrews, as you walked to the first tee area, I noticed you carrying your bag. Are you aware that you must have a caddy to play in the tournament?"

"Oh, I am an amateur and I have always carried my own bag," JD responded.

Looking at him, the starter smiled and somewhat gently replied, "That may be, Mr. Andrews, however, at the Masters, all players, professional and amateur, must have a course-approved caddy."

Overhearing this exchange, Joseph Eldman stepped forward.

"Excuse me, I have caddied in past tournaments and would be available to caddy for Mr. Andrews."

JD turned and quietly explained, "Joseph, I cannot afford to pay a caddy fee."

"You have more than paid a caddy fee. The tickets that you gave to my father, providing him with an opportunity that he could only dream of, is more than enough payment."

JD thanked Joseph and turning to the starter, suggested that he get Joseph a caddy ID and whispered to Joseph to give his ticket back to his father so that his father could bring a good friend as his guest. Joseph, smiling, did just that and picking up JD's golf bag, joined him on the first tee.

With everything settled, JD introduced Joseph to Harold Stone, his playing partner, and the caddies introduced themselves to each other. Before the starter announced that play would begin, he informed JD and Joseph that a traditional white jumpsuit and a tournament green cap, both with the Masters logo, would be brought out to Joseph on the course, so that without delay, play could begin.

Once all of this had been settled, the starter announced Mr. Andrews as the amateur player and Harold Stone, club member, playing as a marker, and asked JD to "Play away."

With that introduction, JD pulled his notebook from his back right pocket. Referring to the note on the first page, he selected his driver, teed his ball, looked down Hole #1 known as 'Tea Olive,' and just as Bobby Jones's notebook read, he hit a perfect drive down the left side of the fairway, approximately 295 yards away. Harold Stone and the starter exchanged a brief look of surprise at the length and accuracy of his drive. Turning back to the task at hand, Harold Stone hit his tee shot and the tournament was underway.

Chapter XIII
First Round Play

When JD's tee shot came to rest, it had found the left center of the fairway. Harold Stone, his playing partner and designated marker for the first round, was surprised at the distance of the drive. Looking at JD, Harold remarked, "That was a fine drive, young man."

Smiling, JD said, "Thanks," and began a brisk walk down the fairway. Joseph matched JD's walk stride-for-stride. Harold Stone and his caddy had to hurry to keep up.

Referring to his pocket notebook, he reviewed Bobby Jones's comment that, *for the second shot, go for the middle of the green, setting up a possible birdie putt.* Returning the notebook to his right rear pocket, he pulled the nine iron from the bag. Joseph didn't say a word and figured that if JD wanted any advice about club selection, he would ask. Stepping back, Joseph watched one of the smoothest, easiest swings that he had ever seen. The ball left the club with a solid sound and came to rest right in the middle of the green. With two putts, JD had his par and seemed, at least to Joseph, to be at ease and very comfortable with his game.

From that point on, JD played at an excellent pace. Harold was pressed to keep up and often wondered what his young opponent kept referring to with his notebook. Joseph, on the other hand, matched his pace and was very impressed with his player's calm manner and excellent golf swing.

After getting pars on #2 'Pink Dogwood' and #3 'Flowering Peach,' the players arrived at #4, named 'Flowering Crab Apple.' JD smiled at the name, because, as he was looking down the fairway of the first par 3-hole, he noticed a palm tree.

Asking Joseph about it, Joseph replied that, "It is the only palm tree on the course."

Turning back, JD slipped out his notebook and referring to the comments about this par 3 hole, he read, *Tough downhill shot. Take a long iron, hit to center front between bunkers if pin up front.* The pin was up front, so he took his 3 iron and with a smooth, even-tempo swing, he stuck the shot four feet left of the pin. Making his putt for a birdie 2, he left the green one under for the first four holes. Walking toward the tee box of #5, named 'Magnolia,' JD noticed Joseph's father, Herman Eldman standing off to the right. With a wave of his hand and a big smile on his face, he acknowledged Mr. Eldman. Joseph noticed the genuine affection that JD displayed toward his father and felt a deep, warm, friendly feeling for him. That was a surprise. How a young man from up north could affect him so profoundly was somewhat puzzling. Putting those thoughts in the back of his mind, he turned back to doing whatever he could to help JD play the course. So far, however, he hadn't asked him for any advice, he just referred to his notebook, selected a club and hit the shots. Joseph was amazed that someone who had only played a couple of practice rounds could play with such confidence and skill.

Playing holes #5 'Magnolia,' #6 'Juniper,' and #7 'Pampas,' in even par, JD stood on the #8 'Yellow Jasmine' tee box and read from his notebook, *Jasmine looks wide open, be careful. Play tee shot right center fairway, lay second shot back 60-70 yards then go for the pin with a wedge.* JD executed the shots perfectly, made a six-foot birdie putt, and walked off 'Jasmine' two under for his first eight holes.

Completing #9 'Carolina Cherry' in par, Harold Stone, JD's marker, noticed that they had played the first nine holes of Augusta National in less than two hours, one hour and 40 minutes to be exact. A pretty remarkable pace for a major tournament, even more amazing to Harold was the fact that this young man had played the first nine two under par, scoring a 34.

Making the turn, playing the back nine with the same pace, referring to his notebook before each shot and each putt, JD and his marker, Harold Stone, finished the 18-hole round in three hours and 40 minutes. Not only was the round a quick one, but Harold was somewhat dazed by the fact that this young man had played the round with two more birdies on the back nine and no bogeys for the 18. This four-under round was astounding, especially for a sixteen-year-old amateur.

After shaking hands and thanking Harold for his company, they both turned and walked to the scorer's tent. After verifying JD's score, it was officially posted.

Once this task was completed, JD left the scorer's tent and looked around for Joseph.

Noticing him standing off to the side, he approached him and said, "Thank you, Joseph, for carrying my bag."

Joseph smiled, "You're very welcome, JD. I will clean the clubs, store them in the bag room, and be ready to go in the morning."

They both agreed to call Emery at the bag storage area to find out the tee-time for day two and meet an hour and a half before. That would allow sufficient time to hit shots on the range and put in some time on the practice putting area to prepare for round number two.

Thanking Joseph again for his service, JD walked over to the concession stand area and purchased an egg salad sandwich for 75¢, a Coca-Cola for 15¢, and a Georgia Peach ice cream sandwich for $1. Spending $1.90 for lunch seemed to be a good deal to JD and he enjoyed the fact that he could have it right there at the course.

Once he finished his lunch, with his hands in his pockets, he walked around the area like any other spectator. Taken again with the beauty and magnificence of the total scene, he marveled at how fortunate he was to be there. Later, walking down Magnolia Lane and out the front gate, he returned to his room, showered, and put on a fresh set of clothes. Leaving the youth hostel, he decided to go to the nearby movie theatre and enjoy watching a John Wayne western.

As day one of the tournament came to an end and all of the scores had been posted on the large scoreboard just off of the eighteenth green, JD was four under par; two back of the lead and the press corps started to take notice. All of the talk, however, was about day two and all seemed to take a wait-and-see attitude. The general comment was that this Mr. John Andrews is an amateur and amateurs usually don't even make the cut to play on the weekend.

When the movie ended, JD left the theatre and walked to what had become his favorite diner. After a satisfying meal of southern fried chicken with all the trimmings, he returned to his room and following his usual routine, he made his journal entries, called his grandfather, and told him about his first round and mentioned how satisfied he was to have played so well. Congratulating his grandson, Patrick cautioned JD to stay focused and take each day as it came. Promising his grandfather that he would, he said goodbye.

After preparing for bed, he set his alarm clock for 6 a.m. and fell into a deep, satisfying sleep.

Chapter XIV
Day Two, The Second Round

The alarm clock went off at 6 a.m. JD, sitting up, stretched and decided to take a long hot shower. After dressing for his second round, he picked up the phone and called the clubhouse. When the connection was made, he asked to be put through to Emery in the bag storage area. A minute later, Emery picked up.

"Emery, this is JD, would you be able to tell me what my tee time is today?"

"Good morning, Mr. Andrews, you played well yesterday and have an afternoon time of 1:30 p.m. When should I have your clubs and shoes ready?"

"Thanks, Emery, how about 12 noon?"

"Good enough, Mr. Andrews, I will see you then."

Replacing the phone in its cradle, he decided to walk to the local diner and entering the front door, he gave his favorite waitress, Liz, a cheerful "Good Morning."

Smiling back, she asked, "What will it be today?"

As he took his seat in his usual booth, he responded with, "Same as yesterday, I guess."

Laughing, Liz turned and put in the order.

Feeling a breeze of fresh air, JD looked up to see Caroline walk through the front door. He was surprised to see her walk directly to Liz, give her a hug, and say, "Good morning, Mom."

"What are you doing here, honey?"

"I just thought I would stop to have breakfast on my last day of spring break."

"OK, have a seat and I will be with you in a minute."

As Liz turned to fill a couple of sugar containers, Caroline noticed JD sitting close by. Walking directly to his booth, she sat opposite him and with a big smile on her face, said, "Hello, JD, I really didn't think I would have a chance to see you again."

Looking into her bright green eyes, he was almost at a loss for words, but did manage to respond, "I didn't either, but it is great to see you."

"Well, Caroline, I see it didn't take you long to meet my regular morning customer," said Liz, as she approached the booth.

Caroline laughed, "JD and I shared the bus ride from Asheville and we became good friends, right, JD?"

"Yes, we did, but I am surprised to see you here and find out that Liz is your mother."

Liz responded with, "It's a small world, you never know who you might bump into."

"I took the liberty of ordering breakfast for you, Caroline. I hope you don't mind."

"Oh, thanks, Mom, I'll just sit and visit with JD until it's ready."

Liz served them their food shortly after that and while enjoying their meal, JD and Caroline, once again, shared stories about their lives and the areas where they grew up. Meanwhile, Liz observed the two of them and how well they seemed to get along. She was happy that her daughter was an outgoing young woman and seemed to make friends easily.

Caroline finished her breakfast before he did and got up to leave. Leaning over, she touched his arm, "Good luck on the course today."

Blushing, all JD could say was "thank you" and then she was gone. *Wow*, he thought, *I really do wish she lived near me, back home.*

Finishing his breakfast, he thanked Liz and left the diner. Although it was only 8:30 in the morning, he decided to make the walk to the course and just be a spectator for a while.

The rules did not allow him to walk the golf course before actually playing his round, but he was able to wander the general areas around the clubhouse and just observe the people, watching them as they moved to position themselves for the day's activities.

It was still early, around 9 a.m., and since he wasn't really well-known as a golfer, he was able to wander the grounds with other spectators and just breathe the southern air and take in the beauty of the surroundings.

Walking past the practice area, he was surprised to hear, "Hey, runner up, I see you played well yesterday." Looking over to where the person was who had made the rather rude comment, JD spotted Perry Waldorf IV, the player that he had lost to, the year before, in the U.S. Amateur Tournament. He did not care for Perry's smug, superior attitude, so he just kept on walking. However, Perry couldn't let it go. In a loud enough voice for JD to hear, he said, "You're at the big boys' tournament now, muni-boy. Don't think you can compete with us here."

JD kept walking and pretended not to hear, but inside he was seething. He knew he should just let it go, but right then and there he resolved to give everything he had to play well and prove to the 'Perry's' of the world that he did belong and could play this game as well as anyone.

When 11:30 came around, JD started to make his way toward the bag storage area. Once he saw Joseph, all thoughts of his unpleasant encounter with Perry 'the fourth' seemed to slip away. He called out and walking toward each other, they reached out and shook hands. JD's smile was catching, and Joseph returned it with genuine affection.

"Let's get a sandwich at the concession stand before we get the clubs and head for the practice range," said JD.

"I really am not allowed to do that," responded Joseph. "As your caddy, I am technically an employee here and employees aren't allowed to make purchases."

"Okay, I am, so what would you like for lunch?"

"A BBQ sandwich and a coke would be great."

After making the lunch purchase, he brought the food to the club storage area. Handing Joseph his, they sat with their backs to the building and ate in silence.

Emery noticed them and observed how much at ease JD and Joseph seemed to be and a warm feeling swept over him.

Finishing their meal, JD put his golf shoes and cap on, Joseph picked up the golf bag, and they made their way to the practice range. Fortunately, Perry 'the fourth' was nowhere to be seen.

Selecting a spot at the far end, JD began his warm-up routine. Starting with a pitching wedge, he worked his way through his clubs until he finally began to hit balls with his driver. This process took about 30 minutes. With that part of his warm-up complete, Joseph took the bag and they walked to the practice putting area where JD spent another 30 minutes putting golf balls from various areas, until he was satisfied that his stroke was smooth and unhurried. Handing the putter to Joseph, they turned and walked to the first tee. JD noticed it was 1:10 p.m., which gave them just enough time to see the last player of the group ahead, tee-off.

Promptly at 1:15, he was introduced to his playing partner, an Englishman, Tony Smith.

Shaking hands, they wished each other a good round and JD, being the amateur, was introduced to the spectators as "Mr. Andrews," and because he was an amateur, he would be the first to tee-off.

JD pulled his notebook from his back right pocket, refreshed his mind on how Bobby Jones played this opening hole, replaced the notebook, took the driver from Joseph, and drove his shot right down the middle of the fairway.

Tony Smith took notice saying, "Good shot."

JD responded with a, "Thanks."

Then, taking his driver, Tony Smith hit his shot slightly past JD's ball and with those tee shots, round two began.

Hole-by-hole, they played pretty much even, each having one bogey and one birdie. Approaching the #9 hole, named 'Carolina Cherry,' JD checked his notebook. *Aim for the oak tree in the distance, hit a draw shot right to left and let the ball run down to the bottom of the hill,* Bobby Jones had written.

Following this advice, he hit his drive exactly on that trajectory, finding his ball at the bottom of the hill. Asking Joseph for an eight iron, he hit his best iron shot ever with that club and arriving at the elevated green found that his ball had run into the cup giving him an eagle 2. Walking to the tenth tee, he recorded his eagle score, which gave him a 2 under for the front nine, exactly what he had scored on day one.

Having watched JD refer repeatedly to his notebook, Tony Smith asked him what the notebook was.

JD responded by saying, "It's just reminders about playing each hole."

After teeing-off on #10, 'Camellia,' both men continued to play solid, steady golf. JD's back nine seemed to be a carbon copy of his first round. No bogeys and two birdies. Finishing the eighteen holes, Tony Smith turned in his score of one under par and JD posted another four under, totaling eight under for the combined two-day score.

JD and Joseph shook hands with Tony and his caddy, Peter, and before they parted company, Tony and JD had a brief discussion about how well each other played. Wishing each other continued good play over the weekend, they went their separate ways.

Looking at Joseph, JD said, "Same routine tomorrow?"

Joseph just gave him an okay sign with his right thumb and forefinger.

With that, JD turned and made his way to Magnolia Lane and walked out through the front gate.

Back at the scoreboard, JD's cumulative score of eight under par was posted.

The press reporters took notice and the questions began.

93

Chapter XV
Questions

Steve Price of the *Atlantic Daily* wanted to know, "Who is this amateur, who is eight under par after two days? How can we interview him? Where is he?"

Other reporters – print, radio, and TV – started asking similar questions and soon the questions found their way to Mr. Harold B. Wilkinson III.

Calling his staff together, Mr. Wilkinson expressed his desire to have this low-scoring amateur, Mr. John David Andrews, available to answer the questions that were being asked by the press.

Operating on the assumption that Mr. Andrews was staying on the grounds in the amateur guest quarters, 'The Crow's Nest,' he turned to his assistant and said, "Charles, I need you to go there and ask Mr. Andrews to join us in my office."

Returning to Mr. Wilkinson's office, Charles informed all present that, "The other amateurs do not know where Mr. Andrews is staying, because, in their words, 'he isn't bunking with us.'"

The look on Mr. Wilkinson's face was one of total confusion. Turning to face the entire office staff, he asked in rapid order, "Where is he? Where is he staying? Why is he not with the other amateurs?"

When no one replied to these questions, Mr. Wilkinson gave very explicit instructions.

"Gentlemen, let's get some answers. Who is his caddy? Does he know where and with whom he is staying? Let's start there and see if we can solve what has become a very puzzling situation."

Leaving the chairman's office, Charles went immediately to the bag area. Finding Emery, Charles approached and asked, "Excuse me, Emery, do you know anything about one of our amateurs by the name of John David Andrews?"

"Why yes, Mr. Wareng, he seems to be a fine young man and must be quite a good golfer to be eight under after the second round."

"Yes, well, would you know how I can get in touch with him?"

"Isn't he with the other amateurs?" Emery asked.

"No, and that is most puzzling. We don't know how to contact him and Mr. Wilkinson needs to talk with him. Do you know who his caddy is and is there some way we could talk to him to find out how to reach Mr. Andrews?"

"Sure, his caddy is Joseph Eldman. Just a minute, I have his home number on my desk, I will write it down for you."

Thanking Emery, Charles returned to Mr. Wilkinson's office and handed him the slip of paper containing Joseph Eldman's name and phone number.

Picking up the phone, Mr. Wilkinson dialed the number. The phone was answered by a female voice.

"Hello?"

Mr. Wilkinson responded in kind and asked for Joseph Eldman.

"Joseph is not here right now," he was told.

Mr. Wilkinson, somewhat frustrated, asked, "Are you his mother?"

"Yes, I am. Who is calling?"

"Please excuse me, my name is Harold Wilkinson, and it is very important that I talk to him as soon as possible."

"I will have Joseph call as soon as he comes home."

After giving her the number for his direct line, Mr. Wilkinson thanked her and replaced the phone in its cradle. Turning to his assistant, Mr. Wilkinson instructed him to, "Call Grand Rapids, Michigan, and get in touch with Mr. Andrews's family and see if they can tell us where our young man is staying. Also, ask if he has a phone number where he can be reached."

Returning to his office, Charles started by calling information and asking for a listing for a Mr. Andrews located in Grand Rapids, Michigan. Charles did not know that John David Andrews lived with his grandfather and was unaware that they did not share the same last name. Having no luck with this approach, Charles decided to contact the local Grand Rapids newspaper and when connected, asked to be put through to the sports desk.

When the connection was made, he heard a rather raspy voice say, "Bruce Norton, Sports Editor, what can I do for you?"

Charles went on to explain who he was and his need to contact John David Andrews's family.

After listening to his reason for wanting to contact JD's family, Bruce Norton let him know that, "Young Mr.

Andrews lives with his grandfather, his parents were killed in a car accident when John David was very young."

Charles was stunned at hearing this information and responded with an, "Oh, could you contact his grandfather for us and ask him to call as soon as possible?"

"Certainly, I will track him down and give him your name and number."

Once the phone conversation ended, Bruce Norton turned to his rookie sports reporter, Peter Thornton, and in his raspy voice explained the situation and told him to, "Call Mr. Patrick Davis's house and if there is no answer, go there in person and wait until he shows up."

Handing Peter a slip of paper with Charles's name and phone number, Bruce sent him on his way.

Arriving at the Davis's address, Peter found no one home. So, he knocked on the front door of the neighbor's house. When the door opened, Peter introduced himself, showing his *Press* credentials, and explained that he was looking for a Mr. Patrick Davis.

An elderly woman, standing in the doorway, responded by introducing herself.

"Well, young man, I am Mrs. Clara Nimitz and why exactly do you need to talk to Mr. Davis?"

"I have been sent by my boss to ask Mr. Davis about his grandson, John David Andrews."

Smiling, Mrs. Nimitz invited Peter inside and offered him some milk and cookies, just as she used to do for John David after school while he was waiting for his grandfather to return from work.

Peter, smiling back, accepted the invitation and once he was seated at the kitchen table, he explained why he needed to talk to Mr. Davis.

After listening to Peter's explanation, Mrs. Nimitz understood why there had been some confusion.

Deciding to tell Peter the story, Mrs. Nimitz went through the history of JD's parents, the auto accident that took their lives when he was only three years old. How Mr. and Mrs. Davis were the only surviving relatives and how they took JD into their home and raised him as if he was their son.

She went on with the story about how his grandfather introduced him to the game of golf.

Peter asked, "How did he become so good?"

Mrs. Nimitz explained, "Mr. Davis introduced Andy Van Lear, a golf instructor, who lives close by, to John David. He had observed JD hitting golf shots across the street and had asked Patrick about him. After they met, he offered to help. JD agreed and Andy began to teach him. Over time, JD, under the guidance of Mr. Van Lear, progressed to playing different public courses around the Grand Rapids area."

Mrs. Nimitz, with a somewhat misty-eyed look, also told Peter how JD, after his grandmother died, used to come to her house after school, and how they would visit over milk and cookies until his grandfather came home from work.

She also told Peter that, "Mr. Davis works as a furniture finisher at the Baker Factory just down the road, and he usually gets home around 6 p.m."

Peter, looking at the kitchen clock, which hung just over the sink, saw that it was 4:30.

"Thank you, Mrs. Nimitz, for the milk and cookies and the history of JD and Mr. Davis."

Getting up from the table, Peter said that he would return a little after six.

Chapter XVI

Answers

Peter Thornton made his second trip of the day to the home of Mr. Patrick Davis. Noticing the time was 6:30 p.m. and that there was a light showing through the front picture window, Peter walked up the steps and knocked on the door. When it opened, Peter was looking at a person who could have been anyone's grandfather. Before him stood a man about 5'8" tall with gray hair and a somewhat weathered, yet very friendly, face.

"Hello, Mr. Davis, my name is Peter Thornton. I work at the *Grand Rapids Press* in the sports section and I wonder if I might be able to visit with you for a while to ask you some questions about your grandson and his standing in the tournament at Augusta, Georgia?"

With a warm handshake, Mr. Davis said, "Absolutely, come inside. Would you like a Coca-Cola?"

Peter gratefully accepted and they sat at the kitchen table. After taking a couple of sips, he started explaining why he needed to know where JD was staying and how he had arrived in Augusta, Georgia, alone.

Leaning back in his kitchen chair, JD's grandfather explained.

"As a furniture finisher, I make a nice living, but my resources for a trip like the one my grandson is on are somewhat limited. So, JD and I decided that a Greyhound bus trip and a room at the youth hostel, close to the Augusta National Golf Club, would fit the budget and that is how, and why, JD took the trip south, alone."

Mr. Davis then looked Peter square in the eye and asked, "Why is it so urgent for people to know this?"

Peter answered by explaining that, "At the Masters Tournament, the amateur participants always stay in a special area on the club grounds called 'The Crow's Nest,' but JD has chosen to stay at a youth hostel instead of with the other amateurs and no one knows why."

Looking at Peter, Mr. Davis told him that he and JD did not know about that type of arrangement.

"Amazing. Your grandson is 8 shots under par in what is considered the finest tournament in North America and because of where he is staying, no one has been able to interview him about anything."

Peter stood and forgetting all about giving Mr. Davis Charles Wareng's name and Atlanta phone number, he said, "Thank you, Mr. Davis, for your time, I have to get back to the sports department and report my findings to my boss."

Looking again at the kindly grandfather figure standing in the front doorway, Peter told Mr. Davis that, "With JD's standing in the tournament you will probably be hearing from someone at Augusta National. Especially, if JD has another round under par."

Getting into his automobile, Peter drove directly to the *Press* building. Going immediately to the Sports Department, Peter reported all that he had learned to Mr.

Norton. Thanking Peter for doing such a fine, thorough job of fact finding, Bruce Norton picked up the phone and called the number he had been given to contact Charles Wareng. Once the call went through, he asked to speak with Mr. Harold B. Wilkinson III.

When the chairman of Augusta National came on the line, Bruce explained what they had discovered in their conversation with JD's grandfather.

Hearing this information, Mr. Wilkinson's brow furrowed into a frown and he was wondering how such a situation could have happened.

At that very moment, Charles entered the office with a manila envelope in hand and placed it on the desk directly in front of the Chairman. Startled, Mr. Wilkinson thanked Bruce Norton for his efforts and the information. Hanging up the phone, Mr. Wilkinson looked at the envelope and saw that it was addressed to Mr. John David Andrews at his home in Grand Rapids, Michigan. Looking up at Charles, he asked, "Where was this found?"

Charles explained that a housekeeper found it, just now, wedged between the wall and a filing cabinet in the outer office. Both men then realized that they had a very young, 16-year-old amateur, on his own in Augusta, Georgia, with no assistance whatsoever, providing for himself and to top it off, he just happened to be 8 under par after the first two rounds.

Mr. Wilkinson looked at Charles and told him, "We need to locate young Mr. Andrews and talk to him about being available for media interviews following tomorrow's round." Mr. Wilkinson instructed Charles, "Go to the youth hostel and ask Mr. Andrews to arrive tomorrow an hour earlier than he normally would and ask him to come to my office for a short visit before going to loosen up on the practice range."

Just then, Mr. Wilkinson's direct phone line started ringing. Picking up the phone, Mr. Wilkinson said, "Hello," and heard Joseph Eldman introduce himself saying that he was returning Mr. Wilkinson's earlier call. Thanking Joseph for calling, he explained that they had needed to locate Mr. John David Andrews and had since been able to find out where he was staying. Thanking Joseph again for calling back, they said goodbye. Hanging up the phone, Mr. Wilkinson turned to Charles and told him to, "Go to the youth hostel, talk personally with Mr. Andrews, even if you have to stay all night."

Leaving the grounds, Charles drove directly to the youth hostel. Entering, he approached the front desk and asked the young man on duty for Mr. John D. Andrews. Looking behind the clerk, he observed that it was now 8 p.m.

"Mr. Andrews is out for dinner and most likely a movie. He will probably return around 9:30-10:00 p.m."

"Well, thank you. Could I wait for him in the front lobby?"

"Certainly," the clerk responded and nodding toward the only easy chair asked, "Would you like a coffee or glass of water while you wait?"

"Thanks, but no, I will just wait."

Chapter XVII
Found and Informed

Around 10:15 p.m., JD returned to the youth hostel. Walking through the front door, he noticed the desk clerk nod toward a man sitting in the front lobby. Standing, Charles walked toward JD, extended his hand in a friendly greeting, and introduced himself, reminding him that they had shared a breakfast the previous Sunday at Augusta National's clubhouse.

"Yes, I do remember, and thank you again for your kindness."

"You are very welcome, could we talk for a few minutes?"

"Sure," responded JD.

Sitting at a table in the corner of the lobby area, Charles explained, "The chairman of Augusta National would like to talk to you in the morning before you do your warm-up routine."

"Certainly, it will be my pleasure."

"Could you arrive about an hour earlier than usual, for your visit with Mr. Wilkinson?"

"What is this all about?"

"At 8 under par and being the low amateur after the first two rounds, the media are very interested in interviewing you and Mr. Wilkinson would like to prepare you for the coming storm of questions."

"Okay, I will be there at 10:00 a.m."

Shaking hands, Charles and JD said goodnight. Charles watched as JD walked away.

He then turned to the desk clerk and asked, "Can I use the phone for a local call?"

Calling Mr. Wilkinson, Charles let him know what had happened, how he handled it, what he had told Mr. Andrews, and that he would arrive tomorrow at 10:00 a.m. for their meeting.

Mr. Wilkinson thanked Charles, put down the phone, and started to make some notes for their morning meeting.

After saying goodbye to Charles, JD had gone to his room and spent the next thirty minutes writing in his journal about all that had happened that day. Then, he called his grandfather and Patrick told him about the confusion that had taken place and how members of the press would probably start trying to ask him questions about home and his ability to play so well.

"I think it would be best, JD, to just keep your answers short and to the point." He also told him, "Try to stay focused on your game and if possible, ignore the excitement around you." Patrick then told him, "I love you, JD, and wish you the best with your Saturday round."

Thanking his grandfather, he placed the phone in its cradle and got ready for bed.

Sleep did not come quickly. As he lay there, the thoughts of what had happened that day kept coming back over and over. Finally, he thought about the advice his grandfather had given him and with those thoughts, he was able to drift off into a sound, deep sleep.

Chapter XVIII
Saturday

Altering his usual routine, JD had set his alarm for 7:30 a.m., an hour later than usual. When the alarm went off, he sat up, stretched his arms, put his feet on the floor, and went to use the bathroom. When finished, he dressed and walked to his favorite diner. Smiling, he paused inside the front door and greeted Liz with a bright, "Hello."

Smiling back, she returned the friendly greeting, asking, "Will it be the usual, young man?"

With a short laugh, he said, "Yes," and sat at a booth near the front door. Taking his time, JD enjoyed his breakfast and began to think about his upcoming meeting with, what he had been told, were the 'media.' As he understood it, this would be the sportswriters, radio and TV announcers, and the newspaper reporters.

Finishing his breakfast, he asked Liz, "How is Caroline?"

She responded by touching his shoulder and looking directly into his eyes said, "She is fine and she hopes you continue to play well. She talked about you last night during dinner. You two seem to have made quite an impression on each other."

"She really is fun to be around," said JD. "Tomorrow is the last day of the tournament and then I will be going back to Michigan. So, if I don't get to see her, would you say goodbye for me?"

"I most certainly will."

He then said that he would be back the next day, paid his check, and stepped out into another perfect southern day.

Walking the few blocks to the front gate felt good. The walking always helped him loosen his limbs and stretch his leg muscles.

As he drew near to the entrance, he greeted the front gate guard with, "Hello and good morning, Phil."

Phil returned the greeting asking, "How are you feeling today, Mr. Andrews?"

"Great," he responded and asked Phil for the time.

"It is 9:30."

"Thanks," said JD and with a slight wave of his hand, turned and began walking up Magnolia Lane.

Arriving at the clubhouse, he entered the front door and was greeted by the club receptionist.

JD introduced himself and asked to see Mr. Wilkinson.

Pressing an intercom button, the receptionist announced, "Mr. John David Andrews is here to see Mr. Wilkinson."

Before he had a chance to take a chair, Charles walked into the foyer and greeted him with a handshake and a warm smile. Turning, he escorted JD to Mr. Wilkinson's office.

Mr. Wilkinson was seated behind his desk. Looking up as JD entered, he greeted him with a smile and a, "Good morning, Mr. Andrews, nice to see you again, please be seated."

When he seemed to be comfortable, Mr. Wilkinson picked up a large manila envelope and handed it to him.

Glancing at the front label, JD saw that it was addressed to him. Looking up, he asked, "What is in the package?"

Mr. Wilkinson explained, "Every first-time Masters Tournament player receives an envelope like this and it contains all of the information a first-time guest needs to be able to be comfortable with the club requirements and amenities offered."

Mr. Wilkinson then explained why JD had never received his package and also apologized for such an unfortunate error. After a few moments of silence, he asked JD, "Would you like to move from the Youth Hostel and join the other amateur players staying in 'The Crow's Nest'? This is an accommodation that we always offer our amateur golfers and there is no cost for the duration of their stay during the Masters week."

JD, looking at Charles and Mr. Wilkinson, said, "Thank you for the offer but I would prefer to keep my room at the youth hostel."

When asked why, JD explained, "Growing up, I always had my own room and there is a certain comfort level for me to have that same feeling here."

He then went on to explain, "The room is paid for through Sunday evening and I have a bus ticket for home, leaving Monday in the early afternoon. Thank you for your kindness and concern, but I really don't want to change anything, now that I have a good routine going."

"I can certainly understand that, Mr. Andrews, and thank you for your understanding. Would you be able to stay after the round today to meet the media and answer their questions about your performance in the tournament and also about your personal background and training?"

"Certainly, after Joseph and I are finished with the third round, I will go to the media tent and meet with them, if you, Mr. Wilkinson, will go with me for guidance and support."

Mr. Wilkinson actually beamed with a bright smile and assured JD that he would be delighted to accompany him. With that being agreed upon, JD excused himself and walked out of the clubhouse to meet Joseph, so that they could begin their warm-up routine and get ready for their third round, which was set for a 2:00 p.m. tee-time.

Realizing that they had a couple of hours before they needed to be on the practice range, JD suggested they wander over to the food tent and purchase some sandwiches for lunch. Joseph again mentioned that he was not allowed to be at the concession area, but he did say, "It is going to be a long afternoon and maybe we should each have a couple of sandwiches with soft drinks and top it off with an ice cream treat."

Laughing about his excellent meal plan, JD asked Joseph to, "Wait for me near the club storage area and I will bring the food there."

Having made the food purchases, JD returned and after passing Joseph his boxed lunch, they located a shady area to sit and eat. Watching the crowd of people, JD told Joseph about his morning meeting with Charles and Mr. Wilkinson. After telling Joseph about the envelope that was never mailed, he became very quiet and seemed to be lost in thought.

After a few minutes, Joseph said, "My father and I have been wondering why you had seemed to be alone and somewhat unaware of things at the beginning of the week. This information about not having received the envelope certainly answers those questions."

Looking at JD, Joseph asked him, "How do you feel about all of this?"

Looking directly into his eyes, he said, "Joseph, I feel okay and I'm ready to warm up for a good afternoon of golf."

Smiling, Joseph said, "Let's go to the range and start the warm-up process."

During his warm-up routine, Perry Waldorf IV showed up.

"Well, Mr. Andrews, you seem to have had two good days of golf, probably playing above your ability, don't you think?"

"Maybe I am, Perry, we'll just have to see how it goes today. It is too bad we are not playing together, I would have liked to have played against you again."

With a sour look on his face, Perry 'the fourth' turned and walked away.

Handing JD another club to continue the warm-up process, Joseph asked, "What was that all about?"

After hearing the story, he just shook his head and said, "Don't let him get to you, JD. There seem to be those types of people wherever you go."

"Oh, I know, but I just do not understand why he has to be so arrogant. Must be the way he was brought up." With a shrug of his shoulders, he turned back to hitting balls, completing his usual pre-match routine.

Chapter XIX
Saturday, The Third Round

With their warm-up finished, JD and Joseph, with the bag over his shoulder, made their way to the first tee. Standing off to the left, he once again took the notebook from his back pocket and read his notes for 'Tea Olive,' the name of the first hole.

Once he had been announced, he teed-off for the third round and placed the shot long and straight, giving him a good look at reaching the green in regulation. JD's playing partner, James Dorney, was from the state of Georgia and was playing in his sixth Masters Tournament. After teeing-off, both men with their caddies walked off the first tee together. James attempted to strike up a conversation with JD by asking, "What do you think about the course?"

JD responded with a short statement saying, "I like the course very much."

By the tone of his voice, James realized that this young man was focusing on his next shot and decided to keep conversation to a minimum.

Arriving at their respective balls, JD pulled the notebook, read his notes about where to place his second shot, selected his club and with a smooth swing, hit the ball to the center of the green. Stepping back, he watched James do the same. Both men took 2 putts for their pars and walked to Hole #2 'Pink Dogwood,' which is a par 5 dogleg left.

Selecting his driver, JD struck the ball perfectly. Both James Dorney and his caddy looked at each other with a look that said, "Wow!" Once James teed-off, each man with their caddy walked down the fairway as if they were playing alone. Very little was said between them and Joseph noticed that JD was even more focused on his game than he had been the first two rounds.

The weather was perfect, just as it had been all week, sunny, low 70s with very little wind. This was highly unusual for Augusta, Georgia, during the first week of April. Scoring conditions for the players couldn't have been any better. JD loved it and although Joseph noticed how much he was concentrating on each shot, he also noticed that JD seemed relaxed and was swinging through the ball with an ease that seemed to propel the ball farther than he had done the first two rounds.

Reaching his ball for his second shot on this long par 5, JD once again read his notes, took a three wood from the bag, looked at Joseph and with a slight smile on his face, ripped a shot that seemed to explode off the face of the club. Joseph watched the ball soar toward the second green and was amazed when it seemed to land softly and roll toward the flagstick. When they reached the green, they realized that JD's ball was no more than 6 feet from the hole. Once James had finished putting, JD calmly stroked his ball into the cup for a 2 under par eagle.

Following the second hole, both JD and James Dorney settled into a game that seemed, for both men, to come easily. Each played the next six holes in even par.

Approaching the 9th tee, JD was 2 under par for the round and 10 under for the tournament. James had not birdied any of the first eight holes and remained at a total of 7 under par.

Standing off to the right of the tee box, JD read his notes for #9 'Carolina Cherry.' *Aim right, play a draw off the oak tree in the distance. Hit a draw and try to run the ball to the bottom of the hill.* Replacing his notebook, he took his driver, placed his feet in a draw stance, and hit a perfect shot that came to rest exactly where Mr. Bobby Jones's note said it should. His second shot, up the steep hill, found the green, and he made the putt for a birdie.

Playing to par on #10, both men walked to the #11 tee, 'White Dogwood,' knowing that this next stretch of holes was famously called 'Amen Corner.' With the weather being as nice as it could be and the famous 'swirling winds' of Augusta being perfectly calm, Amen Corner didn't really bother either JD or James. Both players shot par on holes #11, #12 and #13.

Walking to the 14th tee, James remarked, "The course seems to be playing quite easy for a Masters Tournament." After that statement, his game seemed to unravel. By the time they finished, James Dorney had shot four bogeys on the last four holes to fall back to 3 under for the tournament.

JD had maintained his focus and composure and birdied holes #15, #16 and #17 with a par on the 18th to post a 6 under, 66, for the round. Putting him at a total of 14 under for the first three rounds.

After the 66 was posted on the large scoreboard, just off the 18th green, the crowd exploded with applause, realizing an amateur was 14 under par and could possibly be playing in the final pairing on Sunday, with a good chance of becoming the first amateur to ever win The Masters.

Chapter XX

The Media Event

Leaving the tent, where he had verified his third round score, Joseph and JD were greeted by Mr. Wilkinson. Shaking hands, JD turned and introduced Joseph. After exchanging a few comments about JD's play and his overall course management, Joseph excused himself and Mr. Wilkinson asked, "Are you ready to meet the members of the media?"

"I would like to freshen up a bit and possibly put on a fresh shirt."

"By all means, take your time, and if you don't mind, I have a fresh green golf shirt with the Masters logo that you could wear."

Giving him the shirt, he added, "I hope it will bring you luck should you wear it during your final round."

Thanking Mr. Wilkinson for the shirt, JD turned and entered the players' locker room. Once he had washed up, combed his hair, and put on the shirt with the Masters logo, he stepped out into the bright Georgia sunshine and greeted Mr. Wilkinson with, "I'm ready." With that statement, they walked together to the media tent. Entering, JD was somewhat taken aback by the flashbulbs going off. The noise level went up a bit and in the midst of it all, JD looked very much like the young man of 16 that he actually was.

Noticing his reaction, Mr. Wilkinson pressed his arm and quietly whispered, "I will stay at your side and if you are unsure of how to answer a question, just look to me for guidance."

The first question asked was, "How do you explain your remarkable play on your first visit to a course as difficult as Augusta National?"

"I first learned the game from my grandfather and later, I had a very fine golf teacher by the name of Andy Van Lear. They always stressed the importance of reading not only the greens but also the fairways and all that surround them. This was how they taught me course management and I have just relied on those basics, no matter where I have played. So, it was just a matter of learning the course and then trusting what they had taught me about the golf swing."

Following a few more general golf questions, a reporter from *CBS* asked JD, "Is your family with you and where are they staying?"

With that question, all of the people in the media tent were very surprised when they saw him lower his head, take a deep breath, and look up with moist eyes, and answer the question with the statement, "My parents were killed in an auto accident when I was 3-years-old and my grandparents raised me." Explaining further, he mentioned, "My grandmother passed away four years ago and now it is just me and my grandfather."

Everyone who was present was just stunned into silence, until a reporter from a local Atlanta newspaper asked, "Did your grandfather accompany you to the tournament?"

"No, my grandfather works in a furniture factory in Grand Rapids, Michigan, and could not make the trip."

Following up on this question, the reporter asked, "How did you make the trip, did you drive to Augusta?"

"No, I haven't had time to take the driver's training course, so I don't have a driver's license. Because of that, I took a Greyhound bus."

With that bit of information, the media went into a questioning frenzy. Mr. Wilkinson had to ask for order. When quiet returned, he asked for the interview to end with a promise that, "If it is okay with Mr. Andrews, we will issue a complete biography first thing tomorrow." With JD's nod of consent, Mr. Wilkinson ended the interview with more than a few disappointed grumbles coming from the journalists.

Walking out of the media tent, Mr. Wilkinson made the suggestion that, "We should have dinner together at the clubhouse with Charles in attendance, so that he can record the answers on the biography sheet that would have normally been submitted if you had received the package that was supposed to have been mailed and returned prior to the start of the tournament."

Agreeing to meet at 8:00 p.m., JD and Mr. Wilkinson shook hands and then he offered to have Charles drive him to the youth hostel. "It might be easier for you to avoid any reporters if he drives you."

"Thank you, I think you are right, where will I find him?"

"Come with me and we will see to it."

Chapter XXI
JD's Biography

After driving to the youth hostel, Charles dropped him off at the front entrance. JD returned to his room and laid down on the bed. He didn't have a lot of time, since it was already 7:00 pm, but he just needed some quiet time to gather his thoughts and get a little rest. At 7:20, he showered, toweled dry, and put on a pair of gray slacks, white shirt, blue striped tie, and a dark blue blazer. Slipping on his only pair of black dress shoes, he silently thanked his grandfather for insisting that he, "Pack these items, *just in case* he should need them."

He was still silently thanking his grandfather for his thoughtfulness as he walked out onto the street. Carrying his blazer over his arm, he made the very familiar walk to the Augusta National Clubhouse. Presenting himself to the receptionist, he asked for Mr. Wilkinson.

"Good evening, Mr. Andrews, we've been expecting you. Please follow me."

Following the receptionist, JD was led to the dining room.

"Please be seated, Mr. Wilkinson will arrive soon."

After a short wait, Mr. Wilkinson and Charles entered and greeted JD. Both men were surprised and pleased to see that he had 'dressed' for dinner. After sharing a very nice meal of salad, rolls, baked potato, and southern fried chicken, they settled into an easy conversation and effortlessly, covered all of the questions that were on the personal biography sheet.

Once they were satisfied that the background and brief history of his life had been covered, Mr. Wilkinson asked, "Would it be okay to release the information to the press?"

"Would it be all right to wait until I start my final round?"

Smiling, Mr. Wilkinson agreed to hold off on distributing the biographical information.

Thanking Mr. Wilkinson and Charles for their kindness and consideration, JD once again accepted their offer to have Charles drive him to the youth hostel.

Arriving at the front door, he thanked Charles for the ride and walked directly through the lobby to his room. Once inside, he sat on the side of the bed and letting out a deep sigh, realized just how tired he was. Nevertheless, he did take the time to make the journal notes about all that happened and then made the collect call to Grand Rapids. His phone visit with his grandfather was not as long as their previous talks had been. Patrick seemed to sense that JD was very tired and so, he deliberately kept the conversation short.

Once again Patrick told JD how much he loved him and wished him success in the final round. Thanking his grandfather 'for everything,' he hung up the phone, prepared for bed, crawled in, and immediately fell asleep.

Chapter XXII
Media Follow-Up

After the media event ended, the newspaper and television reporters made a concerted effort to contact the sports editor of the Grand Rapids newspaper to learn what they could about Mr. John David Andrews, his grandfather, and his golf instructor, Mr. Andy Van Lear.

With the information that Peter Thornton had provided, Bruce Norton, the Grand Rapids Sports Editor, was well prepared for the calls that he knew were coming. With each call, Bruce informed the caller that he would post the story on that evening's AP wire and that would be where the journalists and TV reporters would find the information they needed.

True to his word, that evening, Bruce Norton posted an in-depth history of John David Andrews and his grandfather, Patrick Davis. The press release covered the tragedy of the automobile accident that claimed the lives of JD's parents, how he was raised by his mother's parents, his only living relatives, his grandfather teaching him the game of golf, and how he eventually introduced his grandson to Mr. Andy Van Lear, a teaching golf professional.

The press release also listed JD's early success in the tournaments he played, from the time he started playing competitive golf right through his qualifying for the Masters by virtue of his runner-up finish in the U.S. Amateur.

It was very early, 6 a.m. Sunday, when the Associated Press released the story. The journalists at Augusta National were once again stunned into silence. After a few minutes, they quietly, almost reverently, asked to see Chairman Wilkinson. When Mr. Wilkinson stepped into the media tent, the question was quietly asked, "When will we be able to interview Mr. Andrews and his grandfather, Patrick Davis?"

Mr. Wilkinson informed the journalists, "You will have to wait until the conclusion of the tournament." He also asked the group to, "Please respect the fact that Mr. Andrews has yet to play his final round and everyone at Augusta National will appreciate your restraint, providing Mr. Andrews some space to prepare, without having to answer a multitude of questions." With that statement, Mr. Wilkinson left the media tent.

Returning to his office, he placed a call to the home of Mr. Robert Tremont Sr., the chairman of the Atlanta-based Coca-Cola Company. When Mr. Tremont picked up the phone, Mr. Wilkinson, a close personal friend, said, "Robert, I have a most urgent request."

He then went on to explain what had occurred over the past week and the fact that they had a 16-year-old amateur playing in the final pairing and asked if he could have the corporate plane fly to Grand Rapids, Michigan, and bring the young man's grandfather, his only living relative, to Augusta National by the end of the tournament.

Assuring Harold that it would be done, they said goodbye. He immediately called his corporate pilot,

Benjamin Harris. Explaining the situation and the urgency of getting Mr. Patrick Davis to Augusta National, Robert asked, "Ben, can you make it happen?"

"Yes, sir, I will see to it myself."

When they had said goodbye, Ben proceeded with the arrangements. Once these were made, he drove to the Coca-Cola airport hangar, and began the flight to Grand Rapids, Michigan.

After his conversation with Robert, Harold Wilkinson contacted Bruce Norton at his home in Grand Rapids and asked if he would be kind enough to explain the need to young Mr. Andrews's grandfather and accompany him to the Augusta National Golf Club.

Assuring Mr. Wilkinson that he would take care of the details, they said goodbye. Bruce then drove to Patrick Davis's home on North Monroe Avenue, sat down with Mr. Davis, and explained all that had been happening at the Master's Tournament. Once Patrick realized that JD was playing in the final pairing, he agreed to accompany Bruce to Augusta. Packing a few items in a small carry case, Patrick and Bruce then drove to the airport for their flight. Patrick could barely contain the excitement he felt at the thought of being there and watching his grandson play in the final round.

Chapter XXIII

Sunday

Opening his eyes, JD did not get out of bed. Instead, he stayed still, lying on his back and staring at the ceiling. Thinking about the coming day and knowing his tee time was mid-afternoon, he really did not have to hurry. Taking his time, he slowly took a shower, brushed his teeth, combed his hair, and dressed for the day. Checking himself in the mirror, he mentally thanked Mr. Wilkinson for the fresh green golf shirt with the bright yellow Masters logo that he had given him the day before.

Although it was late morning, JD decided to have a large breakfast. He walked, once again, to the diner that he had been visiting every morning since arriving in Augusta, Georgia. Upon entering the front door, Liz greeted him with her arms spread wide saying, "Well, well, well, you are in the news now."

Asking what she meant, Liz told him to take a seat in his favorite spot and she would bring him the local newspaper's Sunday morning sports page.

Placing the paper on his table, Liz took his order and left to let the cook know what to prepare.

Picking up the sports page and taking a sip of water from the glass Liz had left, JD began to read about himself.

The article was mostly about how well he had been playing and the fact that as an amateur he was in the final pairing for the last round of the Masters Tournament. Finishing the article, JD looked up as Liz delivered his breakfast. Smiling a big, bright, beautiful smile, she asked JD if she could have his autograph next to the article in the newspaper.

"Sure," JD said.

"Oh, I almost forgot," Liz said. "Caroline wished she could have been here to give you this herself and since she can't, she made me promise that I would give you this good-luck piece to carry with you while you play today. She also wanted me to get your address in Grand Rapids, so that you two might stay in touch by writing each other."

Placing a round, coin-like object into JD's right hand, Liz turned away to greet another customer that had just entered the diner. Looking at the coin, he noticed that both sides had an impression of a horseshoe with the phrase 'double the luck,' which made him smile.

Taking the pen Liz had left on the tabletop, he signed the newspaper with 'Thank you for making my stay here in Georgia something special, John David Andrews, golfer.'

Once he had finished breakfast, JD got up to leave. On the back of the guest check, he wrote his address. Placing a larger than usual tip on the table, he paid his bill, thanked Liz for everything, and walked out into the sunshine with the sound of, "Good luck today," ringing in his ears.

Arriving at the front gate and walking up Magnolia Lane, just as he had done each day since the Sunday prior to the tournament, JD was again struck by the absolute beauty of Augusta National. This time, however, Joseph, his caddy, was walking toward him with a rather serious look on his face.

Greeting JD, he told him about the 'buzz' going around concerning the story about JD, his grandfather, and the press release. Asking him how he wanted to handle it, JD responded by saying, "Let's just ignore it, warm up on the far end of the practice range, and get ready for our final round."

"Okay, let's get your bag. You can change into your golf shoes and we can walk to the range together."

They took their time walking to the bag storage area. JD changed into his golf shoes, took one of his golf hats out of his bag, and they left for the practice range. They both noticed a few more cameras taking pictures, but otherwise, no one from the media approached with any questions.

What JD did not know was that Mr. Wilkinson specifically had asked all of the journalists and TV reporters to, "Please respect Mr. Andrews's youth and position on this last day of the tournament and I would appreciate it if you would not approach him or his caddy until the tournament is concluded."

JD and Joseph spent the next forty-five minutes warming up on the practice range and walked over to the putting area to get in some final practice putts before returning to the driving range to hit some balls with his three wood and driver. Finishing their warm-up, they made their way toward the first tee for their 3:00 p.m. starting time.

Chapter XXIV
The Final Round

Arriving at the first tee, JD greeted his fellow player, Wilson Davidson, and his caddy, Brent Hudson. Turning toward the third man, the official starter, JD nodded and greeted him with a smile saying, "Good afternoon, Mr. Wilks, we have another beautiful day here at Augusta."

Mr. Porter Wilks smiled back. "Yes, we certainly have had a most unusual week of calm, sunny weather."

"Well, gentleman, since you are both 14 under par, with Mr. Andrews being an amateur and having finished his third round first, he will have the tee."

Turning toward the people gathered around the tee area, Mr. Porter Wilks announced, "Mr. John David Andrews, playing out of Grand Rapids, Michigan, has the tee. You may play away, Mr. Andrews."

With that announcement, Joseph handed JD his driver and just as he had the first three rounds, he hit the shot perfectly down the left middle of the fairway. Stepping aside, JD watched Wilson Davidson hit his drive down the middle, and the final round was underway.

Walking off the first tee, JD noticed that the crowd of spectators was much larger than the first three rounds. The fact that he was an amateur in the last pairing on the final day of the Masters, had increased the crowd to a size that he had never experienced. Turning to his caddy, he said, "I am going to need your help today."

This surprised Joseph, because for the first three rounds JD had not asked him for any help with club selection, distance decisions, or reading the breaks on the greens. So, the only thing he could say was, "Well, JD, I will do all I can to help. What do you have in mind?"

"Have you noticed the size of the crowd?"

"I have, they are at least six rows deep."

"Well, if you notice me becoming distracted at any time during this round, please stop me from whatever I am doing and remind me to just concentrate on the next shot. I think this could help me today."

Joseph smiled and said, "I can certainly do that and if you need anything else, just ask."

The first hole proved to be uneventful, with both players making routine pars. Checking his notebook, JD read, *Don't miss left off the second tee, aim down the right side of the fairway.* Pocketing his notebook, he took his driver and hit the shot far down the right side. Wilson hit an exact copy of JD's drive and seemed quite pleased as he picked up his tee and strode off the tee box. Both men played the second, third, and fourth holes in even par.

Over the next four holes – five, six, seven and eight – JD shot par on five and seven with a birdie on each of number six and eight. Wilson, however, was playing brilliantly and birdied holes number five, seven, and eight with a par on number six. JD was now one shot behind, being sixteen under par, while his opponent was seventeen under.

Both men shot par on nine and ten. Wilson, looking at JD, remarked, "We have a very good match going, Mr. Andrews. I wonder how the rest of the field is playing."

JD gave a nod and shrugged his shoulders.

Proceeding to the 11th hole, named 'White Dogwood,' JD turned to his caddy and said, "Well, Joseph, this is our last shot at Amen Corner."

This is what the 11th, 12th, and 13th holes at Augusta National had become known as because of their difficulty. When the wind was swirling, as it usually was this time of year, these three holes did present a considerable challenge. However, for reasons unknown, this year there were no swirling winds and really, no wind at all. Just a slight, gentle breeze.

Taking his notebook from his back pocket, JD read, *Always aim right of the eleventh green as it is guarded by a water hazard, left. Also, remember all putts break toward Rae's Creek.* With those reminders, he proceeded to birdie this long par four, but so did Wilson, leaving JD still one down.

Standing on the #12 tee 'Golden Bell,' a course official asked both JD and Wilson Davidson to wait because the players ahead were looking for lost balls due to a couple of wild shots on both twelve and thirteen. He also informed them that they were waiting for a rules interpretation on Hole #12.

JD realized this could take up to 30 minutes, so looking at Joseph with a mischievous grin, he challenged him to a rock skipping contest on Rae's Creek, just in front of the green. Leaving the bag of clubs at the twelfth tee, they walked swiftly to the water, found some suitable stones, and began skipping them lengthwise down the creek. Oblivious to the people around the area, they did not notice that some of the media were watching. The press picked up the story and reported what they were doing and then the TV crews caught it live. The TV commentators remarked, "Why not? Anything to pass the time during a long delay."

After about 20 minutes, JD and Joseph returned to the twelfth tee, and JD started swinging his eight iron to loosen up for his upcoming tee shot.

While he was swinging his club, one of the course officials approached to give the go ahead and resume play.

JD was curious as to what had taken so long and asked the official what had happened.

"Well, we had a most unfortunate incident. One of your fellow amateurs, a Mr. Perry Waldorf, hit an errant shot off of the twelfth tee and then, when he thought he found it, actually hit a ball that was not his. The mistake was not discovered until he hit his next tee shot and addressed the ball for his second shot. His ball happened to be close to the other player's ball and the other player noticed it was not the ball that Mr. Waldorf had been playing. This was cause for a ruling and resulted in an immediate disqualification of Mr. Waldorf. He did not take the ruling well and tried to claim that it was his original ball. His playing partner, however, is a highly respected professional and the rules official accepted his testimony over that of Mr. Waldorf. After he was escorted off the course, a marker had to be located and brought out to finish the round with the professional."

Walking over to Joseph, JD whispered into his ear, "It seems that Perry has discovered that what goes around, comes around."

"Yes it does, JD."

Once "resume play" was announced, JD and Joseph demonstrated a remarkable ability to refocus on the game. JD proceeded to par #12 and birdied #13 to level his match with Wilson.

Looking up, JD noticed a scoreboard and remarked to Joseph that, "The other players do not seem to have gained any ground on either Wilson or myself and, in fact, most seemed to have slipped back a couple of shots."

Joseph, looking at JD, didn't see any change in the determined look on his face, so he didn't say anything and just followed him to the fourteenth tee box. Both players shot par and proceeded to 'Firethorn,' hole number 15.

JD's notes said, *Bomb the drive right to left. With a good drive, the green can be reached in two.* The tee shot was one of his best and set him up for a second shot that could reach the green. The three wood that he used for his second shot was not his best and he found the ball short of the pond that guarded the front area. With the 15th being a par 5, he felt he could still score a 4 giving him a birdie to maybe go one-up on his opponent.

Checking his notebook, he read, *This is a very flat green, which slopes one-way, back to front.* Selecting his wedge, JD struck his ball crisply and watched it roll past the hole. The ball seemed to stop momentarily, but then rolled back into the hole, giving him an eagle three. This was the one time that Joseph saw JD explode with emotion and throw a fist pump to the sky. Once they, and the crowd settled down, Wilson Davidson made a good chip and a great putt for a birdie 4. Walking toward the sixteenth tee, JD was now one up on Wilson with three holes to play. The next nearest player was four back.

Hole #16 is named 'Redbud' and JD's notes said, *Play to the center of this very tricky green. Putt for a two but do not be disappointed with a par 3*. JD hit his shot a little left of center and the ball rolled forward before finding the slope and working its way to the hole. When the ball came to rest, he had a three-foot putt for a birdie. After Wilson Davidson made his par, JD made his birdie, which put him two-up on Wilson, five-up on the next nearest player, with only the 17th and 18th holes remaining.

Hole #17, 'Nandina,' proved to be routine pars for both men, leaving just the eighteenth to be played.

The final hole is named 'Holly' and while standing on the tee, both JD and Wilson took note of the massive crowd. There were people on both sides of the fairway, all the way from the tee area, up the hill, totally surrounding the final green. TV cameras were evident and the noise level seemed to be deafening. They had been aware of the crowds on the previous seventeen holes, but this was almost overwhelming.

Joseph leaned toward JD, reminding him, just as he had at least a dozen times over the back nine, "Just concentrate on the next shot."

Both players, taking deep breaths, hit good tee shots. Their second shots to the green were different. Wilson's ball came to rest nine feet right of the pin while JD's ball struck the surface of the green, left of the pin and then rolled back, stopping just barely off the putting surface.

JD was away and his putt stopped two feet past the cup. Reaching into his right pants pocket, just as he had done on the previous seventeen greens, he marked his ball with the good luck coin that Caroline had Liz give him. He then stepped back and watched Wilson putt. With his ball rolling three feet past the cup, Wilson was still away. After marking his ball, he tossed it to his caddy who gave it a swipe with a towel. Handing it back, he then watched as Wilson made the putt for his par four.

With a calm beyond his years, JD placed his ball on his mark. Picking up the coin, he looked at it and thought of Caroline. With a slight, hardly noticeable smile, he put it back into his pocket.

Looking at Joseph, he winked and calmly stroked the ball dead center for his par and the win.

At that moment, the crowd exploded into a thunderous applause, with cheers, whistles, and shouts of 'Well done!' 'Bravo!' All in attendance realized that an *amateur* had finally won the Masters. Joseph and JD embraced in a spontaneous hug, after which he bent over and took his ball from the cup.

Pocketing the ball, he started to walk off the green to make his way to the scorer's tent. It was at that moment that he saw his grandfather standing at the edge of the crowd. Walking swiftly to him, he threw his arms around his grandfather's neck in a bear hug of an embrace and promptly lost his composure. As the tears poured down his face and his body was racked with sobs, the crowd stepped back, giving them some room to be together.

The live TV cameras were recording the moment and every commentator just watched in silence. The crowd, however, continued to cheer and applaud.

Finally, after a long couple of minutes, they broke the embrace. Wiping his eyes, JD asked his grandfather, "How did you get here?"

Patrick, looking at his grandson with pride and affection, said, "Mr. Wilkinson arranged it."

JD then asked his grandfather to, "Come to the scoring tent with me and Joseph, I have to post my score."

Once the score was confirmed with JD signing his card, his overall score of 267, 21 under par, was posted on the large scoreboard just off the eighteenth green. Again, the roar of the crowd could be heard over the entire area. JD turned to his grandfather, "Stay by my side until we go home."

"I will definitely be with you until we leave, a team of horses couldn't drag me away." Placing his arm across JD's shoulder, they left the scoring tent together.

Chapter XXV
The Ceremonies

Immediately following the confirmation and posting of JD's winning score, Mr. Wilkinson and, for the first time ever, Mr. Robert 'Bobby' Tyre Jones Jr. walked with JD and his grandfather to the Butler Cabin for the formal presentation of the famous Masters Green Jacket sports coat. For the first time, an amateur had won the Masters Tournament. At the request of the tournament founder, Mr. Bobby Jones, the tradition of the previous year's champion presenting the jacket to the new champion was set aside so that history's greatest amateur golfing champion could do the honors. With a great deal of emotion, Mr. Bobby Jones held the coat while JD slipped it on. Looking up he noticed his grandfather's face was wet with tears of joy. Before he allowed himself to embrace his grandfather, he turned to Mr. Jones and Mr. Wilkinson, and thanked both men for their kindness and the great tradition that they had at the Masters Tournament.

After JD and his grandfather embraced each other and their tears had dried, Mr. Wilkinson escorted the group to the press tent for the post-tournament media interviews. The press corps, TV commentators, and the print journalists had all become thoroughly familiar with JD's history and that of his grandfather, so the questions were more about his four rounds of golf and how he played so well having been a first-time tournament participant.

One reporter did want to know what his caddy had kept whispering in his ear on the back nine.

Smiling, JD told him that Joseph kept telling him to, "Just concentrate on the next shot."

Once the questions were over, Mr. Wilkinson thanked everyone present and suggested that JD and Patrick join him for a lemonade inside the clubhouse, "To let the crowds disperse before they said their goodbyes."

Exiting the media tent, JD spotted Joseph standing off to one side with his clubs. Excusing himself, he walked over and embraced Joseph, thanking him for carrying his clubs during the tournament. "I wish I were able to pay you, Joseph."

"It was my pleasure, JD, besides, you gave my father his lifelong wish of being able to attend all four rounds. Not only that, but his son and his player won the tournament. It doesn't get any better than that."

After another embrace, he and Joseph looked at each other with genuine affection. Joseph told JD, "I will have Emery get your clubs ready for when you leave."

Then JD took off his golf hat, borrowed a pen from a nearby official and autographed the underside of the bill with, 'To Joseph Eldman, my caddy and friend, who helped me win the Masters, J.D. Andrews.' He then turned and gave Joseph the hat. With that, they parted company and JD entered the clubhouse, joining the chairman and his grandfather for the lemonade Mr. Wilkinson had offered.

The refreshments turned into a light supper with Mr. Wilkinson, his assistant Charles, JD and his grandfather enjoying a peaceful hour-and-a-half of unwinding from the stresses of the tournament and, in JD's case, playing in the Masters.

Following the light meal, Mr. Wilkinson let them know that Mr. Robert Tremont had generously offered to fly them back to Grand Rapids, whenever they would be ready.

Looking at each other, both JD and his grandfather said, "Yes."

"I do have to collect my clubs and shoes and I will need to stop at the youth hostel for my clothing. Also, I would like to sign my other golf hat and drop it off at the diner where I have been eating my breakfast every morning since last Monday." He really wanted to leave something for Caroline.

Charles then stepped forward and offered to drive and make the stop at the hostel and diner before delivering them to the Coca-Cola airport hangar.

Making a light comment, Patrick Davis looked at his grandson and remarked, "It sure beats the bus."

Everyone laughed and Mr. Wilkinson touched JD's arm, asking him to step into the clubhouse living room to meet with Mr. Robert Tyre Jones Jr. for a final goodbye.

Greeting Mr. Bobby Jones, once again with a firm handshake, the three men sat across from each other in very comfortable wingback chairs.

Mr. Bobby Jones started the conversation by expressing his great pleasure in having an amateur win the tournament that he and Mr. Clifford Roberts founded in 1934.

"If you don't mind telling me, how is it possible that an amateur golfer who has never played our course, except for a couple of practice rounds, could know how to play it so well?"

Looking directly into Mr. Bobby Jones's eyes, JD, with a bright expression on his face, responded, "Last Sunday, while I was waiting for Mr. Wilkinson to return for breakfast, I sat at the desk in the library. Looking for a pen to make some notes in the journal my grandfather had given me, I found a small notebook in the back of the top drawer that was handwritten and titled, 'How I Play the Course' by Bobby Jones. After looking through a few pages, I realized that these notes could help me understand the golf course a little better. So, I wrote some of your comments in my journal about how you thought each hole should be played."

JD then told Mr. Jones and Mr. Wilkinson that, "The notebook is still in the desk drawer and I hope you don't mind that I used it for some course knowledge research."

With the conversation over, JD stood and shaking each man's hand, he thanked them for all they had done to make his stay at Augusta National so remarkable.

Turning toward the front door and the waiting automobile that would take JD and his grandfather to the airport, he left the room with the sound of Mr. Bobby Jones's hearty laughter and his comment of 'Well done, young man.'

www.ingramcontent.com/pod-product-compliance
Lightning Source LLC
Chambersburg PA
CBHW061735050726
47598CB00002B/491